More Than Mee

She had knocked and scratche ... ng the night, but he didn't answer, figu ... was her. Later he started to hope that it hadn't been Debra. The daughter was pretty and young, but the mother was lovely and ripe. He wouldn't have turned her away, despite the fact that she was married. It was obviously not a happy marriage.

As he got closer he could see there were two of them, swaying in the slight breeze. As he got even closer, he started to worry, hoping that it wasn't who he thought it was. If it was, he was going to have to go back to town and he hated going back, especially when he thought he had left someplace behind.

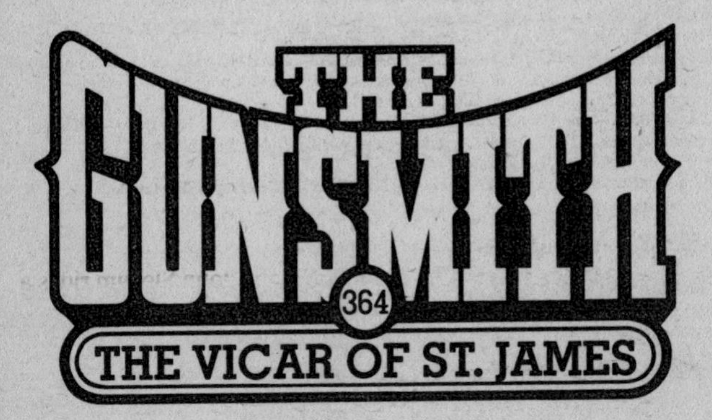

J. R. ROBERTS

JOVE BOOKS, NEW YORK

THE BERKLEY PUBLISHING GROUP
Published by the Penguin Group
Penguin Group (USA) Inc.
375 Hudson Street, New York, New York 10014, USA
Penguin Group (Canada), 90 Eglinton Avenue East, Suite 700, Toronto, Ontario M4P 2Y3, Canada
(a division of Pearson Penguin Canada Inc.)
Penguin Books Ltd., 80 Strand, London WC2R 0RL, England
Penguin Group Ireland, 25 St. Stephen's Green, Dublin 2, Ireland (a division of Penguin Books Ltd.)
Penguin Group (Australia), 250 Camberwell Road, Camberwell, Victoria 3124, Australia
(a division of Pearson Australia Group Pty. Ltd.)
Penguin Books India Pvt. Ltd., 11 Community Centre, Panchsheel Park, New Delhi—110 017, India
Penguin Group (NZ), 67 Apollo Drive, Rosedale, Auckland 0632, New Zealand
(a division of Pearson New Zealand Ltd.)
Penguin Books (South Africa) (Pty.) Ltd., 24 Sturdee Avenue, Rosebank, Johannesburg 2196, South Africa

Penguin Books Ltd., Registered Offices: 80 Strand, London WC2R 0RL, England

THE VICAR OF ST. JAMES

A Jove Book / published by arrangement with the author

PRINTING HISTORY
Jove edition / April 2012

ISBN: 978-0-515-15059-9

JOVE®
Jove Books are published by The Berkley Publishing Group,
a division of Penguin Group (USA) Inc.,
375 Hudson Street, New York, New York 10014.
JOVE® is a registered trademark of Penguin Group (USA) Inc.
The "J" design is a trademark of Penguin Group (USA) Inc.

PRINTED IN THE UNITED STATES OF AMERICA

10 9 8 7 6 5 4 3 2 1

ONE

Father Joseph was the first vicar of St. James, a church that had been built only a few weeks before. The odd thing to Clint, as he rode into the town of Griggsville, Illinois, was that he knew Father Joseph as Joe Holloway, and the last time he'd seen Holloway he'd been carrying a gun, not a Bible.

Clint had received the telegram from Holloway while relaxing in Labyrinth several weeks earlier. "Father Joe" was going to be presiding over the first wedding in St. James Parish, and he wanted Clint to be present. Clint had not seen Father Joe—or Joe Holloway—in years, so his curiosity caused him to accept the invitation to the wedding of two people he did not know. He wondered how they would feel when he showed up.

The parishioners in St. James Parish had already begun to call their vicar "Father Joe."

"Father Joe?"

The vicar looked up from his pulpit and saw Dan Carter, the groom-to-be, standing there. Carter was no youngster—in his thirties—but he was shifting from one foot to the other nervously, as if he were twenty.

"What can I do for you, Dan?" Joe asked. "Are you so anxious that you're here a day early?"

"I'm anxious," the man said, "but I ain't early. I just wanted to talk to ya for a minute."

"Of course," Father Joe said. He stepped down from the pulpit and pointed to a pew. "Do you want to sit?"

Carter had his hat in his hand, and was crushing it mercilessly.

"N-Naw, I don't wanna sit," he said. "Father . . ."

Father Joe decided to let the man get to it on his own. Newly ordained in his forties, he was not yet sure how to handle his parishioners when they came to him for help. Griggsville had never had a church, and the same was true for Joe Holloway, so they all had some learning to do.

Father Joe also noticed that Carter was wearing a gun in church. That was unusual because he rarely saw Carter wear a gun at all.

"Um, look," Carter finally said, "this was a mistake. I'll handle it myself."

As he started to back away, Father Joe said, "Dan, wait. I can help—"

"I'll see you tomorrow, Father," Carter said, "for the wedding," and he hurriedly left the church, almost running.

Father Joe walked to the door and looked out. Carter was moving quickly down the street, jamming his hat back on his head, looking around him nervously. Carter owned the hardware store in town. There was really no reason for him to wear a gun at all, let alone in church. He was a well-liked member of the community, and the wedding was slated to be well attended by his family and friends.

Whatever was bothering Dan Carter, Father Joe hoped the man was able to resolve the issue in time for the wedding.

He turned and went back to the pulpit, where he had been mentally going through the ceremony for the next day's wedding. He was nervous enough about his first ceremony without letting Dan Carter's attitude add to it.

Griggsville was a small town, so Clint didn't feel the need to ask anyone for directions to the church. He rode past the sheriff's office and the hotel, then a saloon, before he came within sight of the church. At that moment a man came out, almost running. Clint reined his horse in and watched.

The man moved swiftly away from the church, frantically looking around him. He was wearing a gun but made no move for it.

At the same time, he saw another man come to the door. From the collar he knew the man was a priest or vicar, or pastor, whatever they called it here. The man watched the fleeing man for a brief moment, then went back inside.

Clint had not seen Joe Holloway for years, but from what

he saw—a tall, square-shouldered man with a full head of hair, albeit gray—he was pretty sure it had been him.

He rode to the church and dismounted, loosely lopped Eclipse's reins over a hitching post. He could see into the church and right straight along the central aisle. The priest was now in the pulpit, looking down in concentration.

"Last place I ever expected to see you," Clint said aloud as he stepped to the door.

TWO

The man looked up from what he was doing, saw him, and smiled. It was the smile that did it. The white collar may have been odd, but this was Joe Holloway.

"Clint! You came!"

Holloway just about leaped down from his pulpit and charged up the aisle. Clint met him halfway, and they hugged tightly, slapping each other on the back.

"Odd to see you without a gun, Joe," Clint said. "Don't you feel a little naked?"

"I did for a while," Holloway said, "but I got used to it."

"And the collar?"

Holloway touched it and said, "Yeah, I got used to this, too. You just get in?"

"Just now," Clint said. "My horse is outside."

"Well," Holloway said, "we'll get you both taken care of. But first let me show you the church."

Clint looked around and said, "I can pretty much see

it from here." He could also smell the recently cut wood that had been used to build it. "Who did the carpentry?"

"The whole town," Holloway said. "They all pitched in."

"They must've really wanted a church."

"They did. It's a small town, but it's gonna grow, and the bedrock of their society is their faith."

"A lot of towns start out that way, Joe. Or should I call you Father Joe?"

"Up to you," Holloway said. "That's what they call me around here—and I'll have none of your cynicism, old friend. Leave it at the door."

"Done!" Clint agreed.

"I have an office in the back," Holloway said, "and a little sacrificial wine."

"I'd prefer a beer."

"We can do that later," Holloway said. "I've been waitin' for you to help me toast the church."

"Let's do it then," Clint said.

As they walked up the aisle, he asked, "What happened with that fellow I saw running out of here? You must have put the fear of Jesus or the Devil into him."

"Honestly, I don't know what happened," Holloway said. "He came to talk to me then abruptly changed his mind. Just about ran out of here. I hope he's okay, because it's his wedding I'm officiating tomorrow."

"He's the groom? Well, that explains it then. Cold feet."

"Maybe," Holloway said as they entered his small office. "But cold feet wouldn't cause him to carry a gun."

"He doesn't usually?"

"No," the vicar said. "He owns the hardware store, and

I've never seen him wear a gun before. And he wears it like he's never worn it before."

"Well, you'd know," Clint said.

They closed the door. Holloway got out the wine and two glasses, poured a bit in each.

"So, Joe," Clint asked, "does the town know your background? Your past?"

"No," Holloway said. "They only know Father Joe, who came to town to be their parish vicar. And I want to keep it that way."

"Your secret is safe with me."

Holloway passed Clint one of the glasses.

"Here's to St. James," he said.

"And Father Joe," Clint said. "May they be a good match."

They both drank.

"Come on," Holloway said, "let's get your horse taken care of, and then get you set up in the hotel. How long were you figurin' on stayin'?"

"Just for the wedding," Clint said. "Tonight and tomorrow night, I guess."

"Always on the go, huh?"

"Actually, not as much as I used to be," Clint said. "I've been known to stay in Labyrinth, Texas, for a spell, which is why your telegram caught up to me there."

They walked back along the center aisle, and then out into the street.

"Quiet town," Clint said.

"A hardworking town," Holloway said. "You only see people walking the streets in the morning when they're going to work, and in the evening when they're going home."

Clint grabbed Eclipse's reins and they started walking up the street.

"Well, I hope the town's faith doesn't keep them from having a decent saloon."

"Depends on what you mean by decent," Holloway said. "There's beer and whiskey. No gamblin', and no whores."

"Well then," Clint said, "I guess I'll just have to make do with the drinking."

THREE

Father Joe stayed with Clint from the livery stable to the hotel, then agreed to meet him later at the saloon.

"I still have some preparations to make for tomorrow," he said.

"Don't worry," Clint said. "I can entertain myself at the saloon."

"I'll see you in about an hour," Father Joe said.

Clint spent some time getting cleaned up from the ride, then left the hotel wearing a clean shirt. He decided to take a walk around Griggsville and finish up at the saloon.

It was a bit later now and there were a few people on the street. Some nodded to him or said hello; others eyed him warily. Apparently they weren't used to having strangers in town.

He was about to head for the saloon when he spotted the hardware store across the street. Remembering that Father Joe had said the groom owned it, he crossed over and found it open. He stepped inside. The store was cluttered, but seemed to have everything in the way of hardware you might need.

What it didn't have was someone working behind the counter.

"Hello?"

He walked around, figuring the man might be hidden among the clutter, but no luck. He risked a look in the back room, but all he found was even more clutter. The store seemed deserted.

He stepped outside, stopped a moment to look around him. There was no one on the street here, and still no clerk for the store. He decided to forget it and headed for the saloon.

The saloon was small, with little space between the tables and chairs. The bar was short, with a single bartender behind it. As promised by Father Joe, there were no gaming tables, and no girls.

He went to the bar, where one man was standing, staring into a beer. He wondered idly if this was the groom.

"Beer," he told the bartender, who just nodded and went to get it.

The man at the bar looked up from his beer and stared at Clint.

"You got a problem?" he asked.

"Me? Nope," Clint said, "no problem at all. You?"

"I got a lot of problems," the man said. "A lot of 'em."

Clint looked at the man's waist. No gun.

"Wouldn't be woman trouble, would it?" Clint asked.

"What?" the man asked, turning his head and squinting

at him. "Women? No, no, nothin' to do with women. I wish I had a woman. I'd be home beatin' the crap outta her."

Clint believed the man. He looked the type. Burly, surly, and Clint wondered who the man would actually try to beat the crap out of when he became drunk enough.

"Well," Clint said, "good luck with your problems, whatever they are."

"One of my problems," the man went on, "is bein' trapped in this one-horse town. What the hell brought you here?"

"I'm just passing through," Clint said. "I stopped to see a friend."

"You got a friend in this town?"

"I do," Clint said. "Father Joe."

"Ah, the vicar," the man said.

"Do you know him?"

"Not well," the man said. "I don't go to church much."

"Any idea what other people in town think of him?"

"I can tell you a lot of the men don't like him," the man said. "Uh, sorry . . ."

"No, no, that's okay," Clint said. "Tell me why?"

"Look around you," the man said. "We used to be able to come here and blow off some steam. Poker, faro, and pretty girls. Now look."

"Not much going on, I admit," Clint said.

"Not much?" the man said. "Try nothin'! Eddie, another beer!"

The bartender came over with a second beer for the man and said, "Carl, stop bad-mouthing Father Joe. He's good for this town."

"Good for the town maybe," Carl said. "Not so good for the menfolk hereabouts."

The bartender was about to say something else when the batwings opened and Father Joe came in.

"Well, Carl," he said, "holding up the bar again?"

"Just leavin', Father Joe." He picked up his fresh beer and polished off half of it. "Just leavin'."

He nodded at Clint, walked past the vicar, and left the saloon.

"He said he didn't know you very well," Clint said.

"That might be true," Father Joe said, "but unfortunately, I know him all too well."

FOUR

"So he told you," Father Joe said moments later. "I got rid of the girls and the gambling."

"You told me that," Clint said.

"No, I told you there were none," Father Joe said. "I didn't tell you that I got rid of them."

"And the men around here don't appreciate that fact, huh?"

"Not at all," Father Joe said. "But the women, they loved it."

"And they love you?"

"They are among my strongest supporters."

"Well," Clint said, "being handsome doesn't hurt, right?"

"Nobody ever called me the handsome gunfighter," Joe said. "But I put on a collar, and suddenly I'm the handsome vicar."

"Maybe the men don't like that either," Clint said. "The husbands?"

"And boyfriends."

"That's not Carl's problem, though, is it?"

"Carl? He's got a lot of problems, but women isn't one of them."

"That's what he told me. He said if he had a woman, he'd be home beating her."

"That's why he doesn't have a woman," Father Joe said, "because that's how he treats them."

"Fresh beers, Father," the bartender said, putting them down.

"Thanks, Eddie."

"You still drink whiskey, Joe?"

"Oh no," Father Joe said. "I gave up the hard stuff. It used to make me crazy, remember?"

"I remember."

"A beer once in a while," he said, holding his up, "on special occasions."

"And some sacrificial wine."

"Yes," Father Joe said, "and the wine."

A few more men had entered, ordered drinks, and taken them to a table. Clint noticed that the men nodded to Father Joe, but none stopped at the bar near him.

"I stopped at the hardware store this afternoon," Clint said. "Thought I'd take a look at your groom."

"Oh? What'd you think?"

"He wasn't there," Clint said. "Place was pretty cluttered, but your man wasn't there."

"Really?" Father Joe said. "And the store was open?"

"Wide open."

"That's strange."

"You sure this fella wants to get married?" Clint asked.

"Well, he did," Father Joe. "When he and his wife-to-be came to see me, they were both excited about it."

"What's she like?"

"Younger than him," Father Joe said. "About a dozen years. She's twenty-two. Her parents were starting to worry that she'd never get married."

"At twenty-two?"

"Most women are married by then."

"Not in my experience."

"Well," Joe said, "let's say most decent women."

"Hey, Joe . . ."

"No, you're right," Father Joe said. "That was a low blow. I'm sorry, Clint. You've been with a lot of women. Who's to say whether they were . . . well . . ."

"I can say," Clint said. "I can."

Father Joe looked down.

"I'm sorry. I've got to get used to this stuff. Religion. I can't be too hard on people."

"What's she like? The bride?"

"Young, like I said, pretty. Difficult for her parents to handle."

"In what way?"

"Well, for a long time all she wanted to do was leave town," Joe said. "But now . . . she's happy to get married and have children and raise them here. And this is going to be a good place to raise them."

"You'll see to that, huh?"

"I hope so," Father Joe said. "You know, one of the reasons I wanted you to come here, Clint, was to see for yourself."

"See what, Joe?"

"That I've changed," Father Joe said. "You know what I used to be, how I used to be. And you accepted it. But I never could."

"So now you're different."

"Yes," Father Joe said, "yes, I'm different. Now."

"Good for you, Joe," Clint said. "Good for you."

"Look," Father Joe said, "I've got to go and do a couple of home visits. Why don't I come by your hotel in a couple of hours and we'll get something to eat?"

"Sounds good to me," Clint said.

"Good, good." Joe put his beer mug down on the bar, only half finished. "Thanks, Clint. Thanks for comin'."

Clint watched him leave, thinking there was still some of the old Joe Holloway there.

Was he waiting to come out?

FIVE

Clint had a couple of hours to kill. He could do it in his room, reading, but he decided to go by the livery first and check on Eclipse. He wanted to make sure the big Darley Arabian was being properly taken care of.

He entered the livery and found it empty—except for Eclipse, who had been brushed and fed.

"Hey, big fella," Clint said, rubbing his neck. "Looks like you've been taken care of okay."

He checked the horse's legs, just to be sure. Satisfied that his mount was sound, he left the stable. The liveryman still had not returned, but that wasn't his concern. In fact, nobody's problems in Griggsville were his concern, not the liveryman's, not the groom's, not Carl's—not even Father Joe's. Of all of them, he knew Father Joe could take care of himself.

Or at least, he used to be able to.

He started back to the hotel, found himself detouring toward the saloon again.

Why not?

* * *

"Back again?" Eddie the bartender asked.

"Can't stay away from your beer."

"Don't blame you," Eddie said. "At least that's still good around here."

Clint accepted the beer and asked, "What do you mean by that?"

"Well, the vicar's your friend, right?"

"Right."

"Then maybe you can talk some sense into him."

"About what?"

Eddie leaned his elbows on the bar. He looked around, as if checking to see if anyone was listening. The saloon was busier than it had been all day, and no one was paying them any attention.

"This thing he's got about no girls and no gambling," Eddie said. "You know, the town of Clarksville ain't so far from here, and they got everything—booze, girls, and gamblin'. We're gonna lose most of our business to them."

"So what do you want me to do?" Clint asked.

"Talk some sense into him," Eddie said. "Make him see that we need the girls and the gamblin' to keep this town alive."

"The town, or this saloon?" Clint asked.

"Both of 'em," Eddie said. "You can't have a town without a saloon, and I can't have a saloon without girls and gamblin'. It just ain't . . . natural."

"Well," Clint said, "I have to say I agree with you, but why do you need me? If you want to have girls and games, why don't you go ahead?"

"Because Father Joe's got the town council convinced," Eddie said, "and the council controls the sheriff, and if I try to have even one girl workin' in here, or one poker game, they'll shut me down."

"Why don't you move your business to another town? Like Clarksville?"

"Believe me, I'm thinkin' about it," Eddie said. "I figure you're my last hope."

"Well, I'll talk to him about it, see what he says, but I don't think I'll have any influence over him," Clint said.

"As long as you try," Eddie said. "That's all I can ask."

He lifted his elbow from the bar and went to serve another customer.

Clint did actually agree with Eddie. He didn't see how a town would survive without a saloon that gave full service. But who was he to argue with Father Joe? Maybe if the saloon closed, and people started to leave, he'd see sense.

He finished his beer, waved to Eddie, who gave him an encouraging nod, and headed for his hotel room.

He spent some time reading Edgar Allan Poe before he realized it was time to meet Father Joe in the lobby. He put the book aside, strapped on his gun, and went to the door. Before he could open it, though, there was a knock.

He expected it to be Father Joe, but that didn't mean he could get careless. He put his hand on his gun and opened the door a crack. He didn't know the man who was standing in the hall, but he certainly recognized a badge when he saw one.

"Mr. Adams?"

"That's right."

"Sheriff Cal Bricker, sir. Can I come in and talk to you for a few minutes?"

"I don't see why not," Clint said, swinging the door open, "but I've got to meet Father Joe in the lobby in a few minutes."

"I won't keep you," the lawman said, and stepped inside.

SIX

Clint closed the door and turned to face the lawman. He was in his thirties, looked more like a store clerk than a sheriff. Clint decided that he wasn't very experienced at his job. He just didn't stand behind the badge the way a man used to wearing it did. Also, he wasn't wearing a gun. The last man Clint saw try to be a lawman without a gun was Bear River Tom Smith, and that only lasted a few months before he was shot to death in Abilene.

"What can I do for you, Sheriff?"

"Well, I was talkin' to Eddie over at the saloon and he said you were gonna try to talk Father Joe into lettin' him have girls and gamblin'."

"I never said I'd talk him into it," Clint said. "I only said I'd mention it."

"Well, sir, I wish you wouldn't."

"Why's that?"

"Well, Eddie doesn't speak for the rest of the town," Bricker said. "The council is behind Father Joe a hundred percent. One hundred percent. You can, uh, tell him that when you see him."

The sheriff seemed to be getting nervous.

"I wasn't going to do anything but have a conversation, Sheriff," Clint said. "It might not even come up."

"Well, that'd be fine, just fine," Bricker said. "You, uh, plannin' on stayin' in town for very long?"

"No," Clint said, "not long. Just a couple of days."

"I see," Bricker said. "Well, I won't keep you any longer then."

"Can I ask you something?" Clint said.

"Sure?"

"Why don't you carry a gun? How can you uphold the law without a gun?"

"Well . . . that's somethin' else the council—and Father Joe—wanted to try. See, Griggsville's a quiet town. They want me to try to keep it that way without a gun."

"And that doesn't bother you?"

"To tell you the truth, I'm not very good with a gun anyway," Bricker said, "so it suits me fine."

"And you've never had a need for it?"

"Not so far," Bricker said.

"Well, I wish you luck."

Bricker opened the door and said, "You mind if I go down first?"

"Sure, go ahead," Clint said. "No problem."

As he waited, giving the man time to go down and leave, he wondered if the town sheriff was afraid to have Father Joe see him with Clint.

* * *

Clint came down to the lobby and found Father Joe waiting for him.

"Hungry?" the vicar asked.

"I need a good steak. Can you find me one in this little town?"

"I know just the place."

They left the hotel and started to walk.

"You find your groom?" Clint asked.

"No," Father Joe said, "but I wasn't looking for him. It's going to be up to him to show up for the wedding in the morning."

"What about the bride-to-be?"

"Haven't seen her either," Father Joe said. "Same deal. Up to her to show up, and make sure he shows up."

"You think he will?" Clint asked.

"Oh yeah, he will," Father Joe said. "He wants to marry the girl."

"I hope you're right," Clint said. "I don't want to miss the chance to see you in action in your new job."

"I hope I don't disappoint you."

They walked a bit more, and Clint noticed they were coming to the end of town. He didn't think they could go much farther—but they did.

"Where is this place?" he asked.

"It's outside of town but, technically, still in Griggsville. We're almost there."

"I went back to the saloon this afternoon and talked to Eddie," Clint said. "Also had a visit from your Sheriff

Bricker. Had an interesting conversation with each of them."

"Is that so? About what?"

"Well, in part, you."

"What did they have to say?"

"Eddie's concerned about his business holding up without the usual, uh, entertainments," Clint said. "But the sheriff tells me the town council is determined to see through the decision not to have them."

"I see," Father Joe said. "Ah, here we are. Why don't we wait until we each have a nice thick steak in front of us before we discuss it any further?"

"Suits me," Clint said.

SEVEN

The place was in a two-story structure that looked like somebody's house.

"Where some widows turn their homes into rooming houses after they lose their husbands," Father Joe explained, "Mrs. Colton decided to turn hers into a restaurant. She lives upstairs, but the whole downstairs is her business."

"Does she do enough business in Griggsville to survive?" Clint asked.

"The food is so good she gets people from the surrounding areas to come in and eat," Father Joe said. "She does very well."

Father Joe opened the door and they entered. Clint could see what was once a living room was now filled with tables and chairs. The adjoining old dining room was as full but did not look as odd given its former use.

"Father Joe!"

They both turned and saw a middle-aged woman coming toward them.

"Hello, Mrs. Colton," Father Joe said. "I've brought a friend to sample your cooking."

"Well, any friend of yours is welcome, Father," she said. "Come, I have a very good table for you."

Clint didn't see that their table was any different from the others, but Father Joe thanked her as if it had been made of gold.

"I'll bring coffee right out," she promised.

"And we'll have two of your steak dinners," the vicar said.

"Wonderful!"

She hurried away to the kitchen. Other diners looked over at them, and Clint noticed that none had greeted the vicar as they'd passed among them.

"Now," Father Joe said, "what were you saying about the bartender and the sheriff?"

"Eddie just commented to me how he was losing some of his business to saloons in Clarksville, who still offer girls and gambling."

"Well, that's too bad," Father Joe said. "I would've hoped his customers would be more loyal than that. What did the sheriff have to say?"

"He wanted me to know that the town council is behind you," Clint said. "They agree with the ban."

"As they should," Father Joe said. "It's because of the ban that Sheriff Bricker can uphold the law without carrying a gun."

"Yes, I noticed that."

"Have you noticed that very few men in town carry a weapon?" Father Joe asked.

"No, actually, I haven't seen that many men to notice that."

"I would ask you to give up your gun, Clint, but it's not my place. That would be up to the sheriff."

"He didn't try to take my gun," Clint said, "which was just as well."

"I can understand your reluctance," the vicar said. "It was difficult for me to stop wearin' my gun, but I did it."

"And how's that going to work if somebody from your past rides into town?" Clint asked.

Father Joe laughed.

"First off, why would someone from my past ride into Griggsville? It's nowhere. And second," he went on, "would they shoot a man of God?"

"Oh, I think they would if it's someone who remembers Joe Holloway."

"Well," Father Joe said, "I guess I'll just have to deal with something like that if and when the time comes."

Mrs. Colton came with a pot of coffee and two mugs, poured them full for them, and promised their steaks within moments. She seemed very talkative, almost nervously so.

"Joe," Clint said, "why do I get the feeling . . ." He stopped.

"What?" Father Joe asked. "Go ahead, Clint. If you've got somethin' to say, say it."

"I get the feeling that some of these people—the bartender, the sheriff, even this nice lady—are afraid of you."

"If they are afraid," Father Joe said without hesitation, "it's not me they fear, it's God."

Clint didn't know what to say to that.

"But I don't think it's fear you're seein', Clint," Father Joe went on.

"No?" Clint asked. "What is it then?"

"Respect."

Mrs. Colton appeared at that point with steaming plates and set them down. A man at another table seemed upset, possibly because they had been served before him, but he didn't speak up.

He seemed too nervous to.

Or afraid.

EIGHT

Clint was impressed with the food and the steak. As he ate, though, he watched the people around them. He and Joe were the center of attention, but not openly. Rather than stares, they were getting furtive looks. Some of the people quickly finished their meals and left. New diners came in, but while some were seated, others seemed to change their mind and leave when they saw Father Joe and Clint.

Clint had experienced this before, some people preferring not to be around him, just in case there was some shooting, but he didn't think that he was the cause, here. He wasn't the reason folks were leaving; it was Father Joe, who seemed oblivious to the whole matter.

Father Joe talked incessantly during dinner about his plans for his "parish."

"Eventually," he said at one point, "we'll even have a bigger church built."

"But this one is brand new," Clint said.

"Yes, it is," Father Joe said, "and it suits my needs at the moment, but if my plans pan out, we will be needing a larger place to assemble."

"Then what would you do with this one?"

"Probably turn it into a chapel."

"Well," Clint said, pushing his plate away, "you seem to have everything pretty well mapped out."

"I do." He emulated Clint and pushed his plate away. "And I'll make sure everything goes according to plan."

Mrs. Colton put in an appearance, chattering nervously still.

"Was everything satisfactory?" she asked. Clint wondered what she'd do if they said it hadn't been.

"It was wonderful, Mrs. Colton," Clint said quickly. "Very good."

"Yes," Father Joe said, "an excellent meal, Mrs. Colton."

She seemed visibly relieved.

"Wonderful!" she said. "Did you leave room for pie?"

"Oh, yes," Father Joe said. "Definitely pie."

"And more coffee," Clint said.

"I made apple, peach, and blueberry."

"I'll take peach," Clint said. Father Joe chose to have apple.

"Comin' right up," she said.

As she returned to the kitchen, Father Joe—for the first time since they'd arrived—sat back in his chair and looked around.

"See anybody you know?" Clint asked.

"I may be fairly new to Griggsville," Father Joe said,

"but I know the people I need to know. For instance, the mayor was here earlier."

"Was he? And you didn't speak to him? He didn't acknowledge you?"

"Oh, he and his wife left early."

"And that didn't bother you?"

"What, that he and some other people left when you and I arrived? It's like you pointed out, Clint. They respect what I represent."

"Which is God."

Clint had noticed that several diners had come in and again, upon seeing him and Father Joe at their table, had turned and left.

"Yes," Father Joe went on, "and if they're uncomfortable with the condition their souls are in, then they don't want to talk to me. So they look away, or leave." He shrugged. "That is their problem."

They finished up their pie and coffee, and by the time they were done, the rest of the diners had virtually cleared out.

When they'd finished eating, they complimented Mrs. Colton, who seemed very happy with their praise, but Clint thought she was probably just happy that they were leaving.

"She's an attractive window," Father Joe said as they left. "Too bad."

"About what?"

"I doubt she'll find a suitable husband in this town," the vicar said.

"Do you think she's looking for a husband?" Clint asked.

"Probably not."

"What about you?" Clint asked. "Are you looking for a wife?"

"I'm ordained, Clint," Father Joe said. "I'm not a preacher, who can take a wife."

"Oh, I see," Clint said. "Vow of chastity and all that?"

"Exactly."

"I guess that's one reason why I'll have to remain a sinner," Clint said.

"Not somethin' to joke about, Clint," Father Joe said. "Shouldn't joke about your immortal soul at all."

NINE

In his room Clint kept trying to read, but found he could not concentrate. His thoughts kept going back to Joe Holloway, who was now Father Joe. He was afraid that the only difference between the two might be their collars, and their weapon of choice.

Joe Holloway was a gunman, a fast gun for hire who had killed many men—most of them face to face. No one had ever come close to beating him to the draw.

Father Joe seemed to be wielding his Bible with as much deadly accuracy as his gun. He had people in town afraid of him, and that was something he was used to.

Joe Holloway may have thought that as Father Joe he was a changed man, but Clint was not sure of that. Father Joe may have thought that people were afraid of him because he represented God, but the fact was they were afraid of him.

That was nothing new. Joe Holloway was used to being

feared. So used to it that, even in his new life, he would depend on it.

Clint rose the next morning and dressed for a wedding, putting on his last clean shirt. He strapped his gun on, knowing he'd be the only man in church wearing one.

He found a small café across the street to have a quick breakfast, and then walked to the church for the wedding.

Adele Whittington looked at herself in the mirror. She and her family could not afford a wedding dress. Even if they could have, they would have had to ride to Clarksville or beyond to have one made. She did, however, have a veil, and she now regarded herself through it.

Twenty-two, and considered by her mother and father—especially her father—to be an old maid. Her mother was only thirty-nine, still a lovely woman despite the hardships of being married to Bill Whittington, who was fifty-five. Whittington was a stubborn man who refused to believe the ground when it told him nothing would grow. He worked his hands to the bone, and those of his wife, to prove the ground wrong.

Now he was giving his daughter to a man who ran a hardware store, and had no ambitions beyond that. Adele looked at her hands. At least she wouldn't be working them to the bone in an attempt to prove the ground wrong.

Her mother came in and stood behind her, hands on her shoulder.

"You're beautiful," she said.

"Not as beautiful as you, Mother."

"Oh, my," her mother said, "if only you could see yourself as I do."

"If I'm so beautiful, why is this the only marriage proposal I've ever had?"

"My dear," her mother said, "if we lived in Saint Louis, or Abilene, or Denver, you would have your pick. You'd have a hundred suitors."

"But we don't live there, Mother," she said. "We live here."

Debra Whittington gripped her daughter's shoulders tightly.

"It's time to go," she said. "Everybody's waiting at the church."

Adele got to her feet, turned, and hugged her mother.

"Your groom waits," Debra said softly.

Clint got to the church, saw that every pew was taken. However, there did not seem to be the mood of general elation usually felt at weddings.

He walked down the aisle, saw the vacant looks on the faces of some of the attendees as they stared down. Others looked up at him as he went by, expressionless. If you didn't know better, you'd think they were attending a funeral, not a wedding.

He walked to the door of Father Joe's office and knocked.

"Come!"

He opened the door and went in. The vicar was seated at his desk.

"You made it," Father Joe said.

"I said I would."

The vicar was dressed in black, his white collar almost gleaming.

"The bride and groom aren't here yet," he said.

"What time is the wedding supposed to be?"

"Eight thirty."

"It's eight twenty-five."

"I know," Father Joe said. He stood up. "We better go out and wait."

Clint opened the door for him.

TEN

As they stepped out, what had been a church humming with soft conversation suddenly became quiet. Father Joe came through the door, then turned and looked at Clint.

"I don't suppose I could convince you to leave that gun behind?" he asked.

"Come on, Joe," Clint said.

"I didn't think so."

Father Joe stepped to the pulpit as Clint stood off to the side. At that point the bride appeared at the door with her father and mother.

Clint couldn't see her face through her veil, but if she looked anything like her mother, she was beautiful. The mother looked hardly old enough to have a daughter who was getting married.

The father had the look of a grizzled farmer, used to having his hands in the ground. He had a permanent scowl on his face, which seemed to be a series not of wrinkles, but of seams.

* * *

Debra Whittington looked down the aisle and saw Father Joe standing at the pulpit. Off to the vicar's left was a man wearing a gun.

"Who the hell is that?" her husband asked gruffly.

"Never mind, Bill. This is your daughter's wedding. Don't start anything."

"I ain't gonna start nothin'."

"Then walk her down the aisle and give her away," Debra said.

"Yeah? To who? Ain't nobody up there to give her to."

Debra realized her husband was right. There was no groom waiting.

"Where is he?" she asked.

"He's not coming," Adele said from behind her veil.

"Of course he is," Debra said. "He loves you. Just wait here and I will talk to the vicar."

She walked down the aisle to join Father Joe at the podium.

"Father, where is Dan?"

"I haven't seen him this morning," Father Joe said. "Haven't you?"

"No, of course not," she said. "The bride and groom are not supposed to see each other before the wedding. Did you speak to him yesterday?"

"I did, but only briefly. He seemed . . . a bit agitated."

"Agitated? About what?"

"I don't know, Mrs. Whittington," Father Joe said. "He didn't say."

"B-But . . . he should be here."

"You are correct," Father Joe said, "he should be."

"Can't we send someone to his hardware store to look for him?" she asked.

"I can certainly ask someone to do that," Father Joe said.

"I can do it," Clint offered.

"No," Father Joe said, "I have someone I can send, Clint."

The vicar stepped down from the pulpit and approached a man in the first pew. He spoke to him, and the man rose and left the church.

"I've sent Gabriel to see if Dan is at his store," he told Debra. "Would you and your daughter like to wait in my office?"

"Yes, thank you, Vicar."

Debra went back up the aisle to get her daughter and bring her into the vicar's office. Her husband left the church and paced back and forth in front.

Clint joined Father Joe in the office with the bride-to-be and her mother.

Adele Whittington sat with her head bowed, still covered by her veil.

"This can't be happening," Debra said.

"I'm sure he'll be here," Father Joe told her. "He's just late."

"I can't have my daughter embarrassed this way," Debra said.

Clint felt bad for the mother and the daughter, but didn't know what he could do to help, so he simply remained silent.

They waited several minutes until there was a knock on the door—a second door, one that led directly to the outside.

"Ah, that will be Gabriel," Father Joe said. He rode and opened the door. He spoke briefly to Gabriel so that the other could not hear, then closed the door with the man still on the outside.

"I'm afraid," he said, turning to the others, "that Gabriel didn't find Mr. Carter at his store. In fact, he says the store was open, and deserted, and he wasn't in his rooms above."

He looked at Clint. They realized that was the way Clint had found the store, and it remained so overnight.

Dan Carter was missing.

ELEVEN

Clint and Father Joe walked over to the hardware store themselves, stopping along the way to get the sheriff. He checked the store, the storeroom, and Carter's rooms upstairs.

"Nothin'," Sheriff Bricker said. "Don't even look like there was a struggle."

"Odd," Father Joe said.

"Maybe," Bricker said, "he just got cold feet. Changed his mind."

"Why disappear, though?" Clint asked.

"Well, you don't know the old man, Ben Whittington. He'll kill Carter for this, if we find him."

Clint and Father Joe exchanged a glance.

"I guess we'll have to tell everyone the wedding's off," Clint said.

"I better do a mass," Father Joe said. "Might as well, while I have everybody in the church."

"That poor girl," the sheriff said. "I wouldn't wanna be the one to tell her and her parents."

"Don't worry, Sheriff," Father Joe said. "That's my job."

They walked back to the church together.

"I don't believe this!" Ben Whittington exploded. "I'll kill 'im."

"You'll have to find him first, Ben," the sheriff said.

"That's your job, Bricker!"

"Not me," the lawman said. "Dan Turner ain't broke any laws, he just didn't show up for his wedding. Seems to me that's a problem for the father of the bride."

"I better go inside and tell the ladies," Father Joe said, "and then the congregation."

"You gonna tell all those people my Adele's been left at the altar?"

"What else can I tell them?" Father Joe asked.

"I'll be humiliated!"

"What about your daughter, Mr. Whittington?" Clint asked. "Don't you think she's the one who'll be humiliated?"

"Ah!" Whittington said. "Go ahead and tell 'em whatever ya want! I need a drink."

He stalked away to the saloon.

Father Joe made a deal with Clint.

"I'll talk to the parishioners, get them to stay for a mass," he said. "Can you talk to the ladies, tell them what we found?"

"We didn't find anything."

"Exactly."

"Yeah, okay," Clint said.

"I'll go into the church," Father Joe said. "You use the back door to the office."

"Is it unlocked?"

"Here." Father Joe gave him a key. "I'll see you after mass."

"How long will that take?"

"An hour."

"What am I supposed to do with the two women?" Clint said. "Keep 'em in your office?"

"Take them somewhere."

"Where?"

"Get them something to drink."

"The saloon?"

"That is a place that sells drinks," Father Joe said. "I'll meet you there."

"All right," Clint said. "I don't know why I'm doing this, but all right."

Father Joe slapped him on the shoulder and said, "You're a good friend, Clint."

"Yeah."

Clint went around behind the church to the back door and used the key to open it. He startled both women as he entered.

"Where is Father Joe?" Debra asked.

"He's in the church starting a mass."

"Then you didn't . . ."

"Didn't find Dan."

Adele had removed her veil. Clint saw that she was every bit as lovely as her mother—or would be when she reached that age. She also looked calm—very calm.

"And my husband?" Debra asked.

"I think he went to the saloon."

Debra looked at her daughter.

"I'm sorry, dear."

Adele shrugged.

"Why don't we go over to the saloon and have a drink?" Clint said. "You can join your husband there."

"Sure," Debra said. "Why not? There's not much that can be done here, is there?"

TWELVE

Clint entered the saloon with the two women and directed them to the bar. Eddie was cleaning the top of the bar with a rag.

"We're not open yet."

"Come here," Clint said, grabbing the front of Eddie's shirt and pulling him to the other end of the bar. "This young woman has just been left at the altar. She and her mother deserve a drink, don't you think?"

"Sure, sure, Mr. Adams," Eddie said.

"Bring them some brandy, and me a beer."

"Comin' up."

Clint rejoined the women and Eddie came over with their drinks.

"Where's the father of the bride?" Clint asked him.

"Huh?"

"Whittington," Clint said. "He headed over here for a drink a little while ago."

"I only just opened the door when you got here," Eddie said. "If he knocked, I didn't hear him."

"Okay, forget it," Clint said.

"I'm sorry about your wedding, Adele," the barman said.

She smiled at him and said, "Thanks, Eddie."

"Go away!" Debra told him.

"Yes, ma'am."

"Don't take it out on him," Clint said.

She glared at him. "I don't want him near my daughter."

"Because he's a bartender."

Clint looked at Eddie, cleaning the other end of the bar. He looked to be a few years older than Adele, but a lot younger than Dan Carter. He was starting to get the picture.

"What's wrong with being a bartender?" Clint asked. "It's a good job."

"You would think so," she said. "You're a man."

"Yes, ma'am, I am."

She drank her brandy, turned to her daughter, and started talking to her in low tones.

"Stop it, Mom," Adele said, pulling away. "I'm fine."

"How can you be fine, when you just got left at the altar?" Debra said.

"Well, maybe I don't care."

"Now, Adele, that's no way to talk."

"Dan's a nice man, Momma, but he's a lot older than I am."

"Your father was a lot older than I was when we got married."

"I know," Adele said, "and look what happened to you."

"I've had a good life."

"Oh, Momma, you're miserable," Adele said. "He treats you so badly."

"He's . . . he's not that bad," Debra said, but she was not convincing.

Clint stood by quietly.

"You can't even convince yourself, Momma," Adele said. "Eddie, some more brandy!"

"Sure, Adele."

He brought two more glasses and set them down. Debra finished the one she was holding and picked up the fresh one. She seemed to be out of arguments.

"So what do we do now, Mother?" Adele asked.

"Finish your drink," Debra said, "and we'll go back home."

"No."

"What?" Debra asked.

"I don't want to go home," Adele said. "Ever. And I don't want you to."

"Adele—"

"Not to him, Mother," Adele said. "He's off somewhere getting drunk. If we do go home, we should pack our things and leave."

"Leave?" Debra asked. "And go where?"

Adele looked around helplessly.

"Well," Clint said, "you could start with the hotel."

"You did what?" Father Joe asked.

Clint and the vicar looked over at the two women, who were now sitting at a back table together.

"I told them I'd take them home to get their things," Clint said. "They want to leave the old man."

"You're going to help a woman leave her husband?" Father Joe asked.

"Well," Clint said, "I figure I'll be helping them stay alive. The old man's bound to be drunk by now."

"Clint," Father Joe said, "I just wanted you to soothe their feelings, not agree to help break up a marriage."

"Afraid it's not much of a marriage, Joe," Clint said. "He beats both of them."

"But that's between him and his wife," Father Joe said.

"Joe," Clint said, "I can't let them go back there alone. You don't want him to murder them, do you?"

"No," Father Joe said, "no, of course not."

"Good," Clint said.

"What will you do?"

"I'll help them get their things," Clint said, "and then escort them to the hotel. Once they're in a room, I'll come and see you."

"And what about the husband? The father?"

"Whittington couldn't get into the saloon, so he's probably off somewhere with a bottle of whiskey."

"And if he's not?"

"I'm not going to kill him, if that's what you mean," Clint said. "I'm just going to keep him from killing them."

"All right," Father Joe said. "See that's all you do, then."

"Don't worry."

"I'll be waiting at the church."

"I'll see you there."

As Father Joe left, Clint walked to the table and said to the two women, "Ladies?"

THIRTEEN

Debra and Adele Whittington had come to town on a buckboard with Ben. The buckboard was still in front of the church. Clint decided to saddle Eclipse rather than ride to their house on the buckboard with them.

He helped both women up onto the buckboard, and then mounted Eclipse. The church was empty, and Father Joe came to the door to watch them ride away.

"Father Joe doesn't approve," Debra said.

"Don't worry about Father Joe," Clint said. "You've got to do what's right for you."

"See, Mother?" Adele said. "Mr. Adams understands."

Debra looked at him, riding alongside them. Adele was handling the reins.

"You seem to be friends with Father Joe," she said.

"I was friends with Joe Holloway," he replied. "I'm not so sure about Father Joe."

"He has the town under his control, you know."

"Whose fault is that?" Clint asked. "You have a town

council and a sheriff. Why would the town let a man with a Bible control them?"

"It's the women," Adele said. "They were so desperate for a priest, and a church, that they welcomed him with open arms."

"There's something about him," Debra said. "He's not like any man of God I've ever known before."

Clint kept silent. Joe Holloway's past was his own business.

When they reached the Whittington house outside of town, it seemed deserted.

"Mr. Adams," Adele said, "if he's here and drunk, you have to be real careful. He'll go crazy."

"Does he have a gun?" Clint asked.

"He has a rifle in the house," Debra said.

"All right," Clint said, dismounting. He looked at Adele. "Put that brake on."

She did so, and he helped both women down, then followed them to the front door of the house.

"Let me go in first," he said.

They stood aside while he entered and determined that the house was empty.

"Okay," he said, stepping outside again. "Pack light and fast."

But of course, by the time they were done, they had the back of the buckboard full, and Clint had to find some rope to tie everything down.

"Did you leave anything?" he asked.

"My mother is entitled to all this," Adele said.

She was, of course, entitled to her clothes, and all the pots and pans she took from the kitchen, but he wasn't sure about the chairs and small tables they'd taken. There was nothing so heavy they had needed his help, so he had stood by and watched them carry things from the house. If he had to, he could swear he hadn't touched a thing himself.

Clint looked around, waiting for the man of the house to come staggering into view, but he never did.

"We're ready," Adele said. She touched Clint's arm. "I want to thank you for your help. Maybe . . . later?" She rubbed his arm, and suddenly she didn't look like such a blushing bride-to-be.

"We better get back, Adele," he said.

She turned to let him put his hands on her waist and hoist her up, but first she pressed her firm backside against his crotch.

Yep, not so blushing.

FOURTEEN

They rode back into town, got the buckboard stored in the livery with a tarp tied down over it, and Eclipse back in a stall with some feed.

Clint walked Debra and Adele over to the hotel, where they checked into one room.

Adele kept walking very close to Clint, even bumping his hip with hers, something her mother seemed completely clueless about.

Once they were in their room, Clint stood outside in the hall and said, "I'll see you ladies later."

"Why don't you lie down, Mother?" Adele said. She pushed Clint out into the hall, closing the door behind her and pressing herself up against him so that there was no mistake about what she was doing.

"Adele—"

"Will you come back later for supper?" she asked. "I mean, what if Papa finds us?"

"I have to go and talk to Father Joe," he said. "I'll come back later."

"What room are you in?" she whispered. "Maybe I can come by later. You know, in case I get . . . nervous."

Clint felt his body responding to the nearness of this young, healthy woman, who did not seem the least bit upset about being left at the altar.

"Adele," he said, "you're very lovely, but you're very young."

"Not so young," she said. "My father considers me an old maid at twenty-two."

"Well, he's an idiot."

"That's what I keep trying to tell Mother."

"You better see to her," Clint said. "I'll be back a little later."

"All right," she said, hooking one finger into his belt, "but don't make me come looking for you."

He opened the door to the room and gently pushed her back in.

At the church he found Father Joe walking the pews. The ex-gunfighter looked up as he entered.

"Just making sure everything is clean," Father Joe said. "You know, no tobacco juice? How did things go at the Whittington home?"

"Fine," Clint said. "The ladies cleaned out the house, and Whittington never showed up."

"That's good."

"But what's going to happen when he gets home?"

"He'll have to sober up first, but then he'll probably get upset and go looking for his family."

"Hopefully I won't be around when that happens," Clint said.

"Are you leavin'?"

"Well, I came to see a wedding, and apparently there isn't going to be one."

"When will you leave?"

"I was thinking about tomorrow morning."

"I appreciate you comin', Clint," Father Joe said. "Maybe you didn't get to see the wedding, but you've seen that I'm a changed man."

"Yes." Clint didn't know what else to say. Argue with the man that he really didn't seem to be very changed at all?

"I can't have supper tonight," Father Joe said. "I have some home visits to make."

"That's okay," Clint said. "I think I might have my hands full tonight."

Father Joe tapped Clint on the chest with his forefinger and said, "See that you behave yourself."

"Oh, yeah," Clint said, "definitely."

"I have to go," Father Joe said. "Why don't you sit here awhile."

"And do what?"

"Oh, I don't know," Father Joe said. "Get right with God?"

"Look, Joe, just because you felt the need—"

"Okay, okay," Father Joe said, "I'll back off. You see to your soul yourself."

He patted Clint on the shoulder and left the church.

* * *

Clint waited a few minutes after the vicar left, and then stepped from the church himself. He felt kind of bad leaving town and letting the women deal with Ben Whittington themselves, but they had probably been doing that for many years. And Adele seemed bound and determined to get not only herself away from her father, but her mother, too.

And if they needed help, didn't they have Father Joe waiting in the wings? Wasn't that what a pastor/priest/vicar or whatever was for?

FIFTEEN

The tree was a long way off, but Clint had seen these things before. He knew what it was way before he reached it.

He'd said good-bye to Father Joe that morning, and left Griggsville without seeing Adele or Debra Whittington again. He was sorry to disappoint young Adele, but if he was going to sleep with one of them, he would have preferred the mother.

She had knocked and scratched at his door during the night, but he didn't answer, figuring it was her. Later he started to hope that it hadn't been Debra. The daughter was pretty and young, but the mother was lovely and ripe. He wouldn't have turned her away, despite the fact she was married. It was obviously not a happy marriage.

As he got closer, he could see there were two of them, swaying in the slight breeze. As he got even closer, he started to worry, hoping that it wasn't who he thought it was. If it was, he was going to have to go back to town and he hated going back, especially when he thought he had left someplace behind.

He hoped the two women hadn't been depending on him for anything more than an escort to and from their house, to gather their belongings. He hoped that when they awoke and found him gone, they wouldn't just go back to the husband.

"Ah shit," he said to Eclipse as he reached the tree. If there was something you never forgot, it was the sight of a man hanging from a tree, even at a distance. This time, there were two of them hanging.

Clint rode up to the two bodies, so he could see their faces, which were facing down. Still on Eclipse, he had to ride up close and lean down to see them.

Dan Carter and Ben Whittington.

The groom-to-be and the father-in-law-to-be, hanging from a tree, dead. He couldn't tell from looking at them if they'd been hanged separately, or at the same time. If it had been at the same time, then somebody had grabbed the groom and held him until they were able to grab the father.

From the way their faces looked, they had both choked to death. They had not already been dead when they were strung up.

Somebody had wanted these two men dead. That meant there had to be a connection between them beyond the fact that Carter was going to marry Whittington's daughter. And if somebody wanted them dead, could the same be true for the women?

He backed Eclipse away from the swaying bodies and

did some thinking. He could just continue riding on, leaving Griggsville and all its problems behind him. But could he leave those two women to be killed? Could he go without knowing what the hell had happened here? Was his curiosity that demanding?

Damn it, yeah, it was. And also his concern for the two women. They at least needed to know that their husband/father was dead, and maybe it would help Adele to know that her groom-to-be had a damn good reason for standing her up.

Or maybe she wouldn't care. After all, she didn't seem so upset, did she?

He thought briefly about cutting the bodies down, but hanging where they were, at least they were safe from critters. They'd still be hanging there when he got back with the sheriff and some men.

He took one last look at the men. They were each hanging from their own branch, and each branch looked solid enough to hold their weight until he returned.

He wheeled Eclipse around and headed back to Griggsville.

He decided to ride to St. James Church first, before going to the sheriff. Maybe Father Joe knew something.

He reined Eclipse in and looped his reins loosely over a rail, then entered the church. Empty, like every time he'd been there except for the wedding.

He walked down the aisle, made his way to Father Joe's door, and knocked. When it opened, Father Joe looked at him in surprise.

"Back so soon?"

"Not by choice," Clint said. "I found Dan Carter and Ben Whittington."

"Together? Where?"

"Just outside of town," Clint said. "Hanging from a tree."

"Dead?"

"Dead."

"Lynched?"

Clint nodded.

"Christ, why?"

"Now, that was something I was hoping you could tell me."

SIXTEEN

Father Joe had nothing to offer, but he agreed to go to the sheriff's office with Clint and talk to Sheriff Bricker.

Bricker looked up and showed surprise as Clint and the vicar walked in.

"Mr. Adams," he said. "I thought you left town this morning."

"I did," Clint said. "Unfortunately I didn't get very far."

"Why not?"

"I found two dead bodies hanging from a tree," Clint said. "Dan Carter and Ben Whittington."

"What?" Bricker got to his feet. "Lynched?"

"Yup," Clint said. "They both choked to death."

"Christ! What did you do with them?"

"I left them where they were," Clint said. "I had no way to get them back to town."

"You left them hanging?" Father Joe asked.

"If I didn't, we'd get back and find half-eaten carcasses."

"The buzzards can still get to them," Bricker pointed out.

"Buzzards," Clint said. He just realized that there were no buzzards circling around the tree, and he mentioned it.

"That means they had probably just been strung up," Father Joe said. "The buzzards hadn't even had a chance to gather yet."

"Well," Clint said, "we better get a buckboard out there and cut them down before the buzzards do find them."

"You're right," Bricker said, coming around his desk. "Let's go."

They not only got a buckboard, but the undertaker as well. His name was Harve Jackson. They used his buckboard and the four of them rode out to the tree. Father Joe rode on the buckboard with Jackson while Clint and Bricker used their own horses.

When they arrived, Sheriff Bricker said, "Jesus Christ."

"Please don't blaspheme, Sheriff," Father Joe said.

"Sorry, Father."

They positioned the buckboard beneath the bodies, then Clint and Bricker took hold of their legs while Harve Jackson cut them down.

They laid the bodies down on the bed of the buckboard and covered them, but first Bricker had the undertaker examine them.

"I ain't no doctor," Jackson said, "but as far as I can see, these men ain't got no other wounds. They was hung to death."

"All right," Bricker said, "let's get these men back to town."

"Just a moment," Father Joe said. He recited a prayer over the dead men, then shook his head. "Who would do this kind of thing?"

"I don't know," Sheriff Bricker said, "but I guess I'm gonna have to find out."

Clint and Bricker mounted up. Jackson and Father Joe climbed up onto the buckboard seat and turned it around. They headed back to town to give Debra and Adele Whittington the bad news.

When they reached town, they stopped in front of the church to let Father Joe off first.

"What are you gonna do, Sheriff?" Father Joe asked.

"I'll help Harve get the bodies into his place, and then I'll have to go and tell Mrs. Whittington and her daughter about Carter and Old Man Whittington."

"Why don't you take Clint with you?" Father Joe said. "He already knows the two ladies."

"Hey, wait—"

"That'd be a big help, Mr. Adams," Bricker said. "Would you?"

Clint hesitated, then figured, what the hell.

"Okay, Sheriff," Clint said. "I'll come along to tell them, but then I'm still leaving town."

"Thanks a lot. I'll go and help Harve and be back here."

"I'll meet you here."

Bricker and Jackson went to unload the bodies, and Clint went into the church with Father Joe.

* * *

In his office, Father Joe took a bottle of brandy from the bottom drawer of his desk. He poured two glasses and handed Clint one. They sat there and waited for the sheriff to return.

SEVENTEEN

"This is horrible," Father Joe said.

"It is."

"You must have been shocked."

"Death doesn't shock me," Clint said. "The things people do to each other don't shock me. They didn't used to shock you."

"I'm not shocked," Father Joe said. "More . . . disappointed. With my parishioners. I guess my sermons haven't hit home."

"Well," Clint said, "maybe not to one person."

"You think one person killed both men and strung them up?"

"Hmm, maybe not."

There was a knock on the office door.

"Come in!"

Sheriff Bricker stuck his head in.

"You ready, Mr. Adams?"

"Ready as I'll ever be," Clint said, standing.

"I'll be here," Father Joe said.

Clint and Bricker walked to the hotel, Clint leading his horse.

"One good thing will come out of this," the sheriff said.

"What's that?"

"These two women can go back home without worrying."

"I guess," Clint said. "Let's see if they look at it that way."

They knocked on the door. When it opened, Adele stood there. She was still dressed for her wedding, only without the veil. The dress was a little worse for wear.

"Clint!" she said, then noticed the sheriff standing there. "Sheriff Bricker. Uh, what can we do for you gentlemen?"

"Is your mother here?" the sheriff asked.

"Yes, she's inside."

"Can we come in?" the lawman asked.

"Of course."

She backed up and allowed them to enter. Debra was sitting on the bed, swung her feet to the floor and stood up when she saw them.

"What's going on?" she asked.

"We have somethin' to tell the both of you," Sheriff Bricker said. "This mornin' Mr. Adams left town, but he didn't get very far."

"What's that got to do with us?" Adele asked, standing by her mother's side. Clint noticed they were the same height, but Debra filled her clothes out more fully than her daughter did.

"I found your husband, Mrs. Whittington, and Dan Carter, Adele."

"Found them?" Debra asked.

"Dead."

Debra gasped and Adele took her mother's hand.

"How?" Adele asked.

"Someone hanged them from a tree."

"Lynched them?" Adele asked. "But why?"

"We don't know."

"By who?" Debra asked.

"We don't know that either," Sheriff Bricker said, "but I'm gonna find out."

"Where are they?" Debra asked.

"At the undertaker's."

Debra looked at her daughter.

"We should go," she said.

"Yes, of course, Mother." She looked at the sheriff. "May we?"

"Sure," the lawman said. "We'll walk you over."

"Thank you."

At the undertaker's the two women went inside to view the dead. Clint and the sheriff remained outside.

"What's your first move going to be?" Clint asked.

"Damned if I know," Bricker said. "I'm not a detective."

"You might want to question mother and daughter

about who the men had run-ins with. Maybe somebody's holding a grudge."

"Anything else?"

"Find out who they were doing business with."

"I don't suppose I could convince you to stay and help me," Bricker said.

"I can't—"

"You sound like you've had experience."

"I have, but—"

"If you stay, we can probably solve these killings together, faster."

Clint hesitated, then said, "I'll stay to ask a few questions, maybe put you on the right track."

"Thank you," the lawman said with great relief. "I appreciate it."

Clint shook his head, wondering if he was going to end up wishing he'd kept riding when he found the bodies.

EIGHTEEN

When the women came back out, the daughter was dry eyed, but the mother was weeping.

"I have to take her home," Adele said.

"No problem," Clint said. "I'll take you."

"I'm gonna ask some questions around town," Bricker said. "See what I can find out."

"Let's get you ladies your buckboard from the livery," Clint said. "Sheriff, we'll talk later and compare notes. Oh, and could you please get me a room?"

"Of course."

The sheriff went inside. As Clint and the women walked to the livery, Adele asked, "So you're staying longer?"

"Just to help find out who killed your father and husband-to-be."

"That's good," Adele said. "Very good."

They drove back to the house, and Adele walked her mother inside. Clint followed them in. There were only a couple of chairs left, and Debra sat in one. Adele turned to face Clint.

"We'll get you some help bringing your things back into the house," Clint said.

"No," Adele said, "it'll give us something to do."

"All right," Clint said, "but before I leave, I'd like to ask you both some questions."

"Not my mother," Adele said. "Let's go out—"

"No," Debra said. "I'm all right. Go ahead, ask your questions."

"This is for both of you," Clint said. "Who would want to kill Carter and Ben?"

"I don't know who'd want to kill Dan," Adele said. "All he did was run a hardware store."

"So you don't know anyone he was having trouble with over the last few days or weeks?"

"No."

"Father Joe says Carter was very agitated the day before the wedding," Clint said. "You don't know why?"

"No," she said.

"Maybe he had cold feet," Debra offered.

"Maybe," Clint said. "What about you, Debra? Who had it in for your husband?"

"Who didn't?" Adele asked.

"What Adele means is, Ben was not a pleasant man. He didn't have many friends."

"What about somebody he was doing business with?"

"What business?" she asked. "This is a hardscrabble farm. The only thing he ever fought with was the ground."

"And us," Adele said.

Clint studied the two women. It seemed as if they would have had a motive to kill Ben Whittington, but could the two women have done it and strung him up? And if so, why kill Carter?

"Okay," Clint said. "I'm going to go back to town. I need you two to think this over, maybe talk to each other. You might recall something valuable."

"What are you gonna do?" Adele asked.

"I'm going to try and help the sheriff find out who did this," he said.

"Will you let us know what's going on?" Debra asked.

"Yes, of course."

"I'll walk you out," Adele said, taking his arm.

Outside she yanked on his arm and said, "I was very angry with you last night."

"Oh, why?"

"You know why. I came to your room and you wouldn't let me in."

He disengaged his arm from her. "I didn't hear you knock."

He walked to his horse and mounted off.

She stared up at him and smiled.

"You're not gonna get off this easy, Clint Adams."

"You better see to your mother, Adele," Clint said. "I'll see you later."

She was standing in front of the house, arms folded in front of her, until he was out of sight.

When Clint got back to town, he first saw to Eclipse's comfort and care, then his own. He went to the saloon for a beer.

"Mr. Adams," Eddie said. "Beer?"

"Yup."

"We heard what happened," Eddie said, although at the moment, he was the only one in the saloon with Clint.

Clint accepted the beer and asked, "You got any ideas, Eddie?"

"About what? Oh, you mean who killed Dan and Ben? Naw, not me."

"Tell me about them."

"They was opposites," the barman said. "Everybody liked Dan, and nobody liked Ben Whittington."

"And you can't think of anyone who disliked Whittington enough to kill him?"

"Maybe one or two fellas, but they'd have nothin' against Dan," Eddie said. "Ain't you lookin' for somebody with reason to string them both up?"

"That we are, Eddie. Seen the sheriff?"

"He was here, askin' me a lot of the same questions you just did."

"Did you give him those one or two names of men who disliked Whittington enough to kill him?"

"Tell you the truth, I think it plumb slipped my mind."

"Well then," Clint said, "suppose you give them to me, and I'll pass the information along."

"So you're stayin' in town?" Eddie asked.

"Just for as long as it takes to find the killer or killers," Clint said. "Now why don't you stop stalling and let me have those names?"

NINETEEN

Clint left the saloon after he finished his beer and went in search of the sheriff. Eddie had given him two names, both men who had played cards with Ben Whittington, and accused him of cheating. When Clint asked Eddie if Whittington had cheated, the bartender said yes—badly . . .

"Ben was no card player," he said, "but he needed money bad. He tried palming a card or two and they caught him."

"Didn't kill him on the spot?" Clint asked.

"Well, I could see him palming the cards from here," Eddie said, "but as bad a cheater as Ben was, them two was bad poker players."

"So?"

"They thought he was cheatin'," Eddie said, "but they couldn't prove it."

"Well then, I'll just have to find out if they decided to do something about it later."

"Good luck."

* * *

Clint found the sheriff in his office, sitting behind his desk, looking bedraggled.

"You know, there might've been a few men in this town who wanted Ben Whittington dead, and there are more than a few who ain't unhappy he's dead, but Dan Carter? I can't find anybody who had a bad thing to say about him."

"I came up with a couple of names from Eddie the bartender, men he thought might've wanted Whittington dead, but I heard the same about Carter."

"What about the women?" Bricker asked. "Did they have anything to say?"

"They weren't very helpful," Clint said. "For one thing, Adele wasn't too anxious to marry Carter. I don't think she wanted him dead, but she wasn't upset when he didn't show up for the wedding."

"What about Mrs. Whittington?"

"I get the feeling if Whittington was alive, she would have gone back to him," Clint said. "Unless her daughter could have convinced her not to."

"I don't know what my next move should be."

Clint sat in a chair across from Bricker.

"Well, for one thing, I'd get out to the Whittington house and have a look around. I might find something useful."

"Like what?"

"I don't know," Clint said. "But I'd wait and let the women settle back in first. And then there's Carter's hardware store. Same thing. Take a look around. Maybe there's a letter, a note, some unpaid bills, something that could be helpful."

"Yeah, okay."

"And you might see about having it locked up when you're done," Clint added. "Or people are going to start helping themselves to hardware."

"It's not that kind of town," Bricker said, "but one or two people might get brave."

"I've got to clean up," Clint said, standing, "and get something to eat."

"You have a room at the hotel. Just pick up your key at the desk."

"Thanks."

"No," Bricker said, standing up, "thank you, for agreeing to stay to help."

Clint headed for the door, then stopped.

"One more thing."

"What's that?"

"Talk to your mayor and your town council."

"About you stayin'?"

"Not about me at all," Clint said. "About the two dead men. Maybe you'll find somebody there with a grudge."

"The town fathers?" Bricker asked.

"You never know," Clint said, and left the sheriff scratching his head.

TWENTY

Clint went to the hotel, collected his key, and made arrangements for a bath. He left his rifle and saddlebags in the room, but took two shirts down with him, figuring he might as well wash them in the bathtub, too.

He had washed the shirts, set them aside to dry, and climbed into the tub himself when the door to the room suddenly opened. He grabbed for his gun, which was hanging on the back of a chair he had set next to the tub, but relaxed when he saw who it was.

"The clerk told me you were takin' a bath," Adele said, smiling. She closed the door behind her.

"They should put locks on these doors."

She was wearing a simple sundress, which covered her for the most part, but there was just a small section that was cut out to show some skin—some creamy, smooth, young skin on her chest.

She stood with her back to the door.

"Don't worry," she said. "We won't be disturbed."

"That's not what I meant."

She laughed and said, "I know, Clint, but it's what I meant."

"Adele, you don't exactly act like a young woman who's been left at the altar."

"Are you kiddin'?" she asked. "I prayed that Dan wouldn't show up. My prayers were answered. It was my father wanted me to marry Dan, not me."

"Why?" Clint asked. "Why did he pick Dan Carter for your husband?"

"I guess maybe Dan reminded him of himself when he was young."

"Meaning Carter would have gotten more like him as he got older?"

"Maybe," she said. "That would be a good enough reason not to marry him. My father was a terrible man—an awful father, and a brutal husband."

"Awful father?" he said. "Did he ever . . ."

"Touch me? No," she said, "he didn't go that far. If he had, I would have killed him myself—and not by hanging him. I would've cut his throat in his sleep."

From the look on her face, Clint believed what she was saying. She might've killed her father at some point, but not by hanging him.

Father Joe stood in front of the crucifix on the front wall of his church and stared. He wasn't seeing it, however. He was deep in thought, thinking that his new parish might already be in danger. With two dead men to deal with, he hoped that the sheriff would be predictable, and that the whole matter would blow over quickly.

But what about Clint Adams?

Maybe it had been a mistake to invite Clint to Griggsville. He'd only wanted him to see that Joe Holloway was gone, and that Father Joe was here. He hadn't expected that Clint would get involved in any town business, and now he was here, helping the sheriff investigate the two murders.

This didn't have to be a catastrophe, though. All he had to do was remain in control.

He walked to his office, entered, and closed the door. He made sure both doors were locked, then walked to a chest in the corner, took a key from his pocket, and unlocked it. When he opened it, the item right there on top was a gun and holster, rolled up. It hadn't been removed from there in a few years.

"I don't want to talk about my father," Adele said. "Or my former husband-to-be."

"Well," Clint said, "we can talk about anything you want, when I finish my bath."

"You know," she said, "that bathtub looks so inviting."

"Adele—"

She started to unbutton her dress. Clint knew he could try all he wanted to be a gentleman, but if that dress came off . . .

"Adele, I'm warning you—"

"Warning me about what?" the young woman asked.

"All I want to do is share the bath with you. Are you gonna be selfish?"

He opened his mouth to reply, but she suddenly peeled the dress down to her waist, and she was half naked. Her breasts were full, with brown, already distended nipples.

She peeled the dress the rest of the way down and stepped out of it. Completely naked, she stepped up to the tub, lifted her leg, and got in.

Clint Adams, the gentleman, left the room as she sat in the tub, sliding her smooth, bare legs alongside his.

TWENTY-ONE

"Where's the soap?" she asked, leaning forward and reaching beneath the water. "Oops! That's not the soap."

"No, it's not," Clint said.

She held his hard cock in her hand and stroked it.

"Mmmm, nice," she said.

"Do you have much to compare it with?"

"More than my parents would think," she said. "Especially my father. He still thinks—thought—I was a virgin."

"And your mother?"

"I've caught her looking at me funny a time or two, like she knew. But she never said anything."

She was stroking him while they talked. She certainly seemed to know what she was doing. Clint wondered how many of the men in town had been with her.

"I've been very discreet," she said as if she could read his mind. "Like I am now."

"You consider this discreet?"

"Nobody saw me come in."

"The desk clerk?"

She smiled. "He won't say a word."

She brought her knees up so she could scoot closer to him. He couldn't help himself. He reached out to take her breasts in his hands, tickle the nipples with his thumbs.

"Mmm, yes," she said. "See how much fun it is when we both play?"

"Where does your mother think you are?"

"Stop worrying about who knows what," she told him, "and enjoy."

She leaned forward and kissed him, a kiss that started tentatively, but then went on and on. The tip of his hard cock broke the surface of the water, and she reacted with delight.

"Oooh, yes," she said, "I was impressed before, but now—"

They kissed again, and he slid his hands along her inner thighs until he was probing her. Her heat was more intense than the heat of the bath as he inserted a couple of fingers into her. She closed her eyes and moaned, her nostril flaring.

"Oh, yes," she said as he moved his fingers, "yes, yes . . ."

"Do you think we could dry off and make it to my room?" he asked her.

"We can dry off, but there's no need to go to your room," she said. "We have all this floor space."

Clint got out of the tub first, then helped her out. He paused to take a look at all of her slippery, wet skin. She let him look, then got down on her knees and took his wet, hard cock into her mouth. This was further proof—rock-hard proof—that she was not the innocent her parents thought she was.

She grabbed his buttocks and sucked him greedily, then pulled him down to the floor with her. It was cold, but neither of them noticed. She rolled him onto his back, then squatted over him and took his cock inside her. She began to ride him, her feet flat on the floor, her thigh muscles working as she slid up and down his slick cock.

"Jesus," he said after a while, "don't you ever get tired?"

"Not when it feels this good," she said. "I could slide up and down on you all day."

"Well," he said, "we don't have all day, so . . ."

He reached for her, grabbed beneath her arms, and lifted her off him, then turned her onto her back. He spread her legs, slid on beneath them, and rammed himself into her. With no give in the floor beneath her, each stroke took him good and deep, and she gasped each time.

"Yeah, oh yeah," she said between gasps.

Well, she'd been pushing him since the day before, bumping him with her hip, touching him with her hands, so she was finally getting what she wanted.

And he wasn't exactly complaining either.

When they were done, they dried off completely and got dressed.

"We should go out separately," he said.

"Worried about my reputation?" she asked.

"Well, it's afternoon now," he said. "We're not going to walk out of here and go unseen."

"I don't care."

"Maybe your mother will," he said. "Don't argue with me. Just wait here for a few minutes and then leave."

"Okay," she said, "but I'll see you later tonight, won't I?"

"We'll have to see," he said. "I'll be helping the sheriff try to find out who killed your father."

"Whoever it is," she said, "when you find him, give him a medal for me, will ya?"

TWENTY-TWO

Clint came out into the lobby as a man and woman were checking in. The man nodded to him, but the woman looked away. They were dressed like Easterners. Clint had the feeling she was afraid of him—and probably afraid of any man she saw in the West.

He went to his room so that he wouldn't be in the lobby when Adele came out.

He left his washed shirts in the room, putting them on the windowsill to dry. When he thought he'd given Adele enough time to get out of the hotel, he went back downstairs. All the exercise he'd gotten with the girl had made him hungry. He decided to walk to Mrs. Colton's and have a good meal.

When he got there, she greeted him warmly and showed him to a table. There were other people eating at a few tables, but they didn't look at him. He didn't know if they were afraid of him because of who he was, or because he was friends with Father Joe.

Mrs. Colton took his order herself and brought him a beautiful steak platter and a pot of coffee.

"You let me know if there's anything else you need, Mr. Adams."

"Well, Mrs. Colton," he said, "I'll need you to call me Clint, if that's okay."

"That's fine, sir," she said. "Uh, Clint, that is. Please, enjoy."

He did. As he ate, he felt the energy he had expended with Adele returning to his body. By the time he got to a piece of pie and another pot of coffee, he was feeling completely renewed.

People came and went around him, and he felt the weight of their stares on him. He did not, however, feel threatened in any way, which suited him. They could stare all they wanted, as long as they didn't try to introduce bullets into his meal.

By the time he was finished, the place had emptied out. He paid his bill and told Mrs. Colton, "I'm sorry if I scared off your customers."

"Oh, don't worry," she said. "You didn't. I usually have a lull about this time, and then they start coming in for supper."

"Still," Clint said, "I noticed all the stares. I don't know if it's because of who I am, or because I'm friends with Father Joe."

"Well," she said, "you wouldn't catch me sayin' anythin'

bad about Father Joe. He's cleaned up this town and a lot of folks don't like it."

"Cleaning up a town is usually the job of whoever's wearing a badge."

"That may be, but Sheriff Bricker didn't do much to accomplish that. Father Joe's only been here a few months, but look at what he's done."

"So you like Father Joe."

She hesitated, then said, "Let's say I approve of what he's done around here."

Clint studied the woman, and decided not to press the question. She obviously did not want to admit whether she did or did not like the vicar.

"Okay, Mrs. Colton," Clint said. "Thanks."

She nodded and went back into her kitchen. Clint let himself out of the house.

He walked to the sheriff's office, found Bricker sitting on a wooden chair out front.

"I didn't expect to find you here," Clint said.

"Then why'd you come here?"

"Good point," Clint said. "You got another chair?"

"Inside."

Clint opened the door, reached in, grabbed the other chair, and sat down next to Bricker.

"What've you got?" Clint asked.

"I've got nothin'," Bricker said. "I'm sittin' here feelin' frustrated."

"Well, you know, you could send for some federal help."

"Like what?"

"A federal marshal."

"Why would the feds send a marshal to this place?"

"Hey," Clint said, "murder is murder. Do you have a newspaper in town? I haven't noticed."

"No newspaper," Bricker said.

"What's the closest paper?"

"I'm not sure."

"Clarksville?"

"Maybe. Why?"

"If these murders get into a newspaper, and then get picked up by other newspapers, the feds might get interested."

"That would take days."

"Probably."

"Are you gonna stay here that long?"

"Well . . . I was kind of thinking you wouldn't need me if you had a marshal."

Bricker thought a moment then said, "I suppose we could start with a newspaper story."

TWENTY-THREE

Clint found Father Joe sweeping the floor of the church.

"You don't have somebody to do that for you?" he asked.

Father Joe stopped, leaned on the broom, and asked, "Are you offerin'?"

"No," Clint said. "I've got enough to do. I'm trying to find a killer."

"Any luck?"

"No," Clint said. "I don't think Debra or Adele did it, but I haven't ruled anyone else out."

"Haven't you?"

"No."

Father Joe stared at him, then shrugged and continued sweeping.

"Yeah, okay," Clint said. "I don't think you killed either one of them."

"Thanks for that."

"I came over to tell you that I'm leaving town for about a day."

"To do what?"

"I have to go to Clarksville and see that these murders get into the newspaper." He explained about getting a federal marshal interested.

"That's sneaky," Father Joe said. "You get a marshal in here and you can leave."

"Exactly."

"If Clarksville has a telegraph office, you could do a lot with that."

"I was thinking about that, too," Clint said. "Send a telegram to the state capital."

"Well then," the Vicar said, "one way or another, you'll be getting help."

"One way or another."

"Want me to come with you?"

"What for?"

"Watch your back."

"With what? A Bible?"

"It's a mighty weapon."

"Not in this case," Clint said. "You stay here and keep an eye on things, Vicar."

"That's my job," Father Joe said. "Keeping an eye on my flock."

"Well then, just keep doing your job," Clint said. "For the time being, I seem to have mine."

Clint stopped by the Whittington house to talk to Debra and Adele.

Adele opened the door to him and smiled.

"You back for more already?" she whispered.

"I just came to talk to you and your mother for a minute."

"Well, come in."

He entered, found Debra sitting in a chair, looking pale.

"I just wanted to let you ladies know I'll be leaving town briefly."

"Where are you goin'?" Adele asked.

"Clarksville, for a start," Clint said. "I'm going to see what I can do about getting some federal help in here to find out who killed your husband. Your father."

"In Clarksville?"

"Maybe," Clint said.

"When will you be back?"

"Maybe tomorrow," Clint said. "I'll check in when I come back."

Adele walked Clint to his horse.

"Kiss me good-bye?" she asked.

"Not here, Adele."

He mounted up and looked down at her. She put her hand on his leg.

"Be careful."

"I'm always careful."

He wheeled Eclipse around and rode away.

The first shot came just as he reached the hanging tree. He cleared the saddle, hit the ground as the second shot sounded. He knew it was from a rifle, from a ways off.

On the ground he scampered over to the tree, using the trunk for cover. He didn't remove his gun from his holster. The shooter was too far away, using a rifle.

He sat with his back against the tree trunk. Okay, he thought, who knew he was coming out here? The sheriff, the vicar, Debra and Adele Whittington. He couldn't imagine either woman out there with a rifle. Joe Holloway could have made the shot with ease. If he was out there, he missed on purpose. Father Joe . . . well, he didn't know about him. And he had no idea what kind of a hand Sheriff Bricker was with a rifle.

But whoever the shooter was, he clearly didn't want Clint leaving town.

Clint decided to give him what he wanted.

TWENTY-FOUR

Clint entered the sheriff's office without knocking.

"Hey!" Bricker said from his desk. "I thought you left town."

Clint didn't reply. He walked to the gun rack on the wall, tried to remove one of the rifles, but it was locked.

"You got the key for this?" he asked.

"Of course," Bricker said, "but do you care to tell me why you want it?"

"I got as far as the hanging tree when somebody took some shots at me."

"Who?"

"That's why I'd like to find out."

"And you wanna check my guns first?"

"Why not? You're one of the people who knew I was going."

Bricker considered for a moment, then took a key from his pocket and tossed it to Clint. He caught it left-handed and used it to unlock the rack. There were three rifles and two shotguns. He left the shotgun where it was, removed each rifle in turn, and sniffed them.

"Satisfied?" Bricker asked.

Clint locked the rack and tossed the key back to the sheriff, who fumbled it, dropped it, and picked it up.

"I'm satisfied that none of these rifles were used."

"So now what?"

"I keep checking."

Clint walked to the door.

"Does this mean you're not leavin' town?"

"That's what it means," Clint said. "Never mind a federal marshal. I'll find this killer myself."

"And what am I supposed to do?"

"Just keep doing your job, Sheriff."

He opened the door and left.

His next stop was the church. He got the same welcome there.

"I thought you left town," Father Joe said as Clint entered the church.

"Somebody changed my mind," Clint said.

"How'd they do that?"

"With a couple of shots," Clint said. "From about three hundred yards away, with a rifle."

"Three hundred yards," Father Joe said. "That's a helluva shot."

"As you can see, they missed."

"And you're back."

Clint shrugged.

"The shooter wants me to stay so bad I thought I'd give him what he wants."

"He?"

"Could be a she, I guess," Clint said.

"But you don't think so."

"No."

"So what's your next move?"

"I checked the sheriff's ordnance," Clint said. "None of it's been fired recently."

"The sheriff?"

"He knew I was leaving town."

"So did I."

"I know."

Father Joe stared at Clint.

"You want to check my rifle?"

"Just to be thorough."

"What makes you think I still have a rifle?"

"Just thought I'd ask."

Father Joe stared at Clint some more.

"Come with me."

He turned and led Clint to the office. He pointed to the chest in the corner.

"Open it."

Clint walked to the chest and opened the lid. He saw the rolled-up holster lying on top.

"Check it," Father Joe said. "Hasn't been fired in years."

Clint closed the lid.

"Not gonna smell the barrel?"

"The shooter used a rifle, not a pistol," Clint pointed out.

"Well . . . that's the only gun I have."

"No rifle?"

"No rifle."

Clint looked down at the closed chest.

"Why keep this one?"

"Old times' sake?"

"Vicar with a gun?" Clint asked.

"I'll get rid of it," Father Joe said, "soon."

Clint shrugged.

"That's up to you. Thanks for talking to me."

"Hey," Father Joe said, "anything I can do to help. I'm right here."

"I'll be in touch," Clint said, and left.

TWENTY-FIVE

Clint thought about riding out to the Whittington house, but if Debra or Adele had taken the shot at him, they'd be back by now, and the rifle they used would be hidden away. So, too, if they had used another man to do the shooting, he'd be hidden or long gone.

He was sure that Adele could have gotten any man to do what she wanted him to do. What he would have liked to do was talk to Debra without her daughter around.

Okay, yeah, that was it. She was the only one he hadn't talked to yet, since the killings. Not alone anyway.

He went to the livery and saddled Eclipse.

As he rode up on the Whittington house, he saw that the buckboard was there, and the horses were in the stable. There was a saddle hanging on the side of a stall. He dismounted and left Eclipse behind the stable, out of sight of the house.

He walked to the side of the house and looked in the

window. Debra was sitting in a chair. It was as if she had never moved since the last time he was there.

Adele was moving about the kitchen, talking to her mother the whole time. She was wearing a simple dress, but not the kind of thing a girl would wear around the house. He thought she was probably going to be leaving soon, so he decided to wait. Maybe she was going to go to town to look for him. That would keep her there for a while, since he wasn't there to find. It would be a while before she gave up looking and went back home.

He settled down to wait.

It took over an hour, and he was about to give up, when she finally went to the front door and opened it.

"I'm just gonna go to town to get a few things," she said to her mother. "I'll be back soon."

He was still watching through the window, but could hear her voice clearly from around the corner. Her mother never moved.

"Bye, Mother."

He moved to the back of the house, hid there, and watched her walk to the stable. It took her a few moments, but she saddled one of the horses and came riding out, headed for town.

He walked around to the front door and knocked on the door. When there was no answer, he opened the door and went inside.

Debra Whittington was sitting in the chair, staring straight ahead.

"Debra?"

She didn't answer.

"Debra, it's Clint Adams."

She looked up at him and smiled.

"I know who you are, Mr. Adams," she said. "I'm not dead, or blind."

"Well, that's good," he said. "I was kind of worried about you."

"Worried? About me? Why?"

"Well . . . I've seen Adele and talked to her, but you don't seem to be leaving the house."

"You're right," she said. "I know you're right. I should get outside. Would you like to go for a walk with me?"

"I'd like that very much," Clint said.

She reached out a hand to him and he pulled her to her feet.

They walked awhile, away from the house and the stable, out where it was green.

"You know," she said, "Ben would never do this with me."

"Do what? Walk?"

"Yes," she said. "Just walk. And Adele, neither would she."

"But you did. You'd walk out here by yourself?"

"Oh no," she said. "Never. If Ben ever thought I was out here just walking, he'd blow his stack. Every waking hour had to be work, work, work."

"Farming is hard work," Clint said.

"Yes, but it doesn't have to be all the time," she said. "All the goddamned time! Does it?"

"No," he said, "I suppose it doesn't."

"Do you know why I've been sitting in that chair in my house all this time?" she asked. "It's because I could. I can, Clint. When Ben was alive, I could never stay still for a minute, or he'd start yelling. Well, he's not around anymore, so I can sit, and I can walk. And you know what else I can do?"

"No, what?" he asked.

She stopped walking abruptly, stepped in front of him, threw her arms around him, and started kissing him.

TWENTY-SIX

They ended up in the house, in the bed, and all the differences between the experienced woman and the talented young girl became evident.

Debra's body was more robust, more succulent, it was . . . more. Her breasts were full and solid, as were her sweet buttocks. She used everything in bed—her hands, her arms, her legs and feet, her mouth, tongue, and teeth. At one point she had his hard cock in her mouth and simply scraped it with her teeth, giving him a combination of light pain and amazing pleasure.

He reveled in her body, exploring it, using as many of his senses as he could, at the same time—sight, touch, smell, oh, and taste. She even tasted better than Adele. It was like the difference between a good brandy and a fine wine—even though he still preferred beer. Debra was like the best beer.

"Oh, God," she said at one point when he was down

between her legs, his tongue avidly lapping at her pussy. "This is something my husband never did."

"His loss," Clint's muffled voice said.

She reached down to hold his head there and closed her eyes . . .

Later she sat astride him, riding him slowly and staring down at him. He watched as her beautiful face became flushed, her eyes glassy, her lips swollen as she bit them. He pulled her down to him to kiss her and swell her lips even more.

Suddenly she stopped and asked him, "What was that?"

"I didn't hear anything," he said.

"Jesus," she said, "I'm so worried Adele will walk in on us."

"You can't stop now," he said. "Not now."

"No," she said, "not now . . . but we've got to finish . . ."

And they did.

They dressed quickly, in case Adele came back too soon.

"My husband and I didn't have sex very much," Debra said as they dressed.

"Like I said, that was his loss."

"You might be wondering about my, uh, experience."

"Debra," he said, "you don't have to explain anything to me. You had a life before your husband, with your husband, and you'll have one after."

"I was lonely a lot," she said. "I was not faithful to Ben. When he left town, I . . . strayed."

They left the bedroom and went back to the main room of the house. She decided to make coffee.

"We need more time," she said. "I kept thinking I heard Adele coming back."

He didn't tell her that he knew when she had left. He didn't want Debra to know he'd been watching them.

"Today is the first day in a long time I've felt alive," she said, sitting across from him at the table, each with a cup of coffee.

"Well, your husband's been killed—"

"That has nothing to do with it," she said. "I've felt dead living all these years with Ben. You brought me back to life today and I appreciate it." She reached across the table to take his hand. "I'd like to show you how grateful, but Adele must never find out."

He squeezed her hand.

"You're the mother, Debra," he said. "You don't have to explain anything."

"If I wasn't afraid she'd be coming back," she said, "we'd still be in bed . . ."

"Don't worry," he said. "There's time. But I need to tell you why I came by here today."

"That's right," she said, sitting back. "I thought you were leaving town."

"I did, but somebody took a shot at me," he said.

"Who?"

"I don't know," he said. "Somebody with a rifle, from a long way off."

She stared at him.

"Did you come here to ask if one of us shot at you?" she asked.

"I talked to the sheriff, and to Father Joe. They both knew where I was going."

"And so did we."

"Yes."

"You questioned the sheriff and the vicar?"

"I did. I checked the sheriff's guns."

"Well," she said, "then I guess there's no reason you shouldn't check ours." She stood up. "We have two rifles."

He knew that. They were hanging up on the wall. She went and got them and brought them back to him, placed them on the table in front of him. He lifted them and sniffed them. Neither had been fired recently—not that day anyway.

"Whose rifles are these?" he asked.

"They were both my husband's," she said. "He hunted with them."

"Do you or Adele shoot?"

"We can," she said. "Ben made sure we learned how, just for protection. But I can tell you Adele was home all day until just a little while ago. She'll tell you that herself about me, too."

Clint took the rifles and hung them back up on the wall.

"I have to go, Debra," he said. "Now I'm not only looking for a killer, but for whoever shot at me."

"When can we be together again?" she asked.

"I'll be in town for at least a few days more," he said. "You can come to the hotel when you can."

"Well, Adele needs me," she said, "but I'll make the time. Now that I've felt alive again, I'm looking forward to doing it again."

"So am I."

She came into his arms and he kissed her, hoping she'd never find out that he'd been with both the mother and the daughter.

And vice versa.

TWENTY-SEVEN

Debra walked Clint outside, waited while he retrieved his horse and walked it to the front of the house. At that point they heard a horse approaching. As he watched, he saw Adele come into view. Obviously she'd determined he wasn't in town, and didn't spend much time looking for him.

"Well," she said, dismounting, "what have you two been up to?" She looked at Clint. "I thought you said you were leavin' town."

Clint hoped Adele wouldn't be able to tell anything by looking at her mother.

"Mother, you're up and around."

"Mr. Adams came to look at our rifles."

"Our rifles? Why?"

He explained to her how he'd been shot at.

"And you think we might have done it?"

"Adele," Debra said. "He checked the sheriff's rifles, and the vicar's gun. Why shouldn't he check ours?"

That seemed to mollify Adele somewhat.

"What did you find?"

"Nothing," he said. "Your rifles weren't fired today."

"And what does that mean?" she asked.

"It means somebody else knew I was leaving town today," Clint said. "I've got to find out who."

He looked at Debra, who still looked kind of sleepy-eyed and swollen to him. She had what a whore had once told him was a "just- fucked" look. Hopefully, Adele was not experienced enough to notice it.

"Debra, did your husband have any friends in the area?" he asked.

"He had more enemies than friends," she said, "but he did have two friends."

"Oh," Adele said, "you're thinkin' of Clem and Delbert."

"Clem and Delbert?" Clint asked.

"Brothers with a farm not far from here," Debra said. "They're about the only ones I could ever think of as Ben's friends."

"I better go and talk to them then," he said.

"I can take you there," Adele said.

"No," Clint said. "We don't know what will happen when I get there. They might start shooting on sight. I'll go by myself."

"He's right, honey," Debra said, touching her arm. "Let him go alone."

"Well," Adele said, "you'll let us know what you find out?"

"I sure will," he said.

They gave him directions to the farm of the Dagen brothers, Clem and Delbert.

"Be careful of them," Debra said. "They're kind of, well, crazy."

"All the more reason Adele should stay here," Clint said.

He climbed onto Eclipse's back and looked down at the two women.

"You ladies better stay close to home," he told them. "It's safer."

He'd slept with both of them, and there was trouble here, but it would be worth it to be with Debra again. There was a lot more to her than he had experienced.

"Be careful," Adele said, and Debra's eyes said the same.

He turned and rode away, wondering what they'd talk about when he was gone.

TWENTY-EIGHT

It was late in the day when Clint came within sight of the Dagen farmhouse. It was nearly dusk, but there were no lights in the house yet. He wondered if they were out somewhere—working, or looking for him to take another shot at him?

But if they were friends with Ben Whittington, and knew that he was looking for whoever killed him, why would they take shots at him?

Perhaps questioning these two brothers—who no one else had mentioned to him—would lead him to the actual killer?

He considered dismounting and leaving Eclipse behind, approaching the house on foot, but in the end he decided to simply ride up to the house and see what happened.

As he approached, the front door opened and a man with a rifle stepped out.

"You jes' hold up right there, mister," he said, pointing

the rifle at Clint. He was a tall, gangly man wearing overalls, with hair that looked like a rat's nest.

Clint reined in.

"No reason for the rifle, friend," he said.

"You let me be the judge of that," the man said. "Whataya want?"

"I'm looking for Clem and Delbert Dagen."

"What fer?"

"I was told that they were friends with Ben Whittington."

"Ben Whittington's dead."

"I know that."

"Then whataya want with us?"

"You're one of the Dagen brothers?"

"I'm Delbert."

"Where's Clem?"

"Right here."

Clint looked behind himself in surprise. Clem—almost identical to his brother—had managed to move up behind him without being heard. He was impressed. Clem also had a rifle pointed at him.

"Glad to meet you, boys," he said. "My name is Clint Adams. Debra Whittington sent me over to talk to you."

"About what?" Delbert asked.

"About who may have killed Ben."

"How would we know?" Clem asked.

"She told me you two were the only friends she could think her husband had."

"Really?" Delbert asked. He seemed pleased.

"She said that?" Clem asked.

"Yes, she did."

The two brothers exchanged a glance and Clint felt they had actually exchanged a thought as well.

"You're the Gunsmith, ain'tcha?" Delbert asked.

"I am."

"You wanna come in and have some mash?" Clem asked.

"Sure," Clint said.

Both brothers lowered their rifles.

"Come ahead, then," Delbert said as Clem joined him at the door.

Clint dismounted, looped Eclipse's reins around a rail, and followed the two men inside. The place smelled like two men who didn't bathe or clean often lived there.

"Set," Clem said while Delbert grabbed a jug from somewhere.

Clint sat at a rickety table, joined there by the two brothers.

"Here ya go," Clem said, handing Clint the jug.

Clint took a swallow of the homemade mash, tried not to choke as the liquid blazed a path down his throat.

"Pretty good," he said.

Clem took the jug back and had two big swallows, then passed it on to his brother, who did the same.

"Whooeee!" Delbert said. "That is good, brother Clem."

Clem took the jug and slammed the cork back into it, but kept it near his elbow.

"What kin we do for ya, Mr. Gunsmith?" he asked.

"Well, you can call me Clint," he said, "and answer a few questions."

"Go on and ask," Delbert said.

"First of all, is Mrs. Whittington right? Were you friends with Ben Whittington?"

"I suppose you could say that," Clem said.

"He come here a time or two to share the jug," Delbert said.

"Don't nobody else we know who wanted to be friends with him," Delbert said, "and nobody else we know who come here to share a jug."

" 'ceptin' you," Clem pointed out.

"Guess that kinda makes us friends with the Gunsmith, huh, brother Clem?" Delbert asked, laughing.

"I guess it kinda does, brother Delbert," Clem agreed.

"Do any of the people in town know that you were friends with Whittington?"

Clem shrugged and Delbert said, "Damned if we know. We don't go to town much. Maybe once or twice a month. We don't talk to many people."

"So nobody but his family knew you were friends."

"We didn't know they knew," Clem said. "Ben didn't talk about his family."

"Not even when his daughter was going to get married?" Clint asked.

"He only said he was finally marryin' her off," Clem said.

"So you knew about it?"

"Sure," Delbert said.

"I didn't see you fellas at the church."

"We wasn't invited," Clem said.

"Why not?"

"We don't like weddin's," Delbert said.

"So you weren't upset about not being invited?"

"Hell, no," Clem said.

"We don't like bein' around people," Delbert said. "And we don't like that vicar."

"Father Joe? Why not?"

"He come out here and tried to make us come to church," Clem said.

"And you didn't like that?"

"Didn't like his way with words," Clem said.

"He jes' about threatened us."

"Said we oughtta come to church, but if we didn't, then he didn't wanna see us in town."

"And is that why you don't go much?"

"Naw," Clem said, "we never gone to town much."

"He didn't scare us none," Delbert said. "But he tried."

"That ain't somethin' a vicar's supposed to do, is it?" Clem asked.

"No," Clint said, "I guess not."

"Damn right," Clem said. He pulled the cork from the jug. "'Nother snort?"

"Sure."

Clint took a drink, passed it back. Clem cleaned the top with his sleeve, took a drink, then passed it to his brother again.

"Did Ben ever mention somebody he was afraid of?" Clint asked. "Maybe somebody he thought wanted to do him harm?"

"You mean somebody who'd wanna kill 'im?" Delbert asked.

"Yes."

"Naw," Clem said. "He never talked about nobody like that."

Clint reached for the jug, uncorked it and took a big swig, handed it back.

"Nobody's being very helpful about this," he complained.

The two brothers exchanged a glance, and then they both grinned.

"What's so funny?"

"We wuz jes' thinkin'," Clem said.

"About what?" Clint asked, wondering how they each knew what the other had in his head.

"Maybe," Delbert said, "you're lookin' for the wrong killer."

TWENTY-NINE

"What do you mean?"

"Well," Clem said, "we're just a coupla dumb shit-kickers . . ."

". . . but we think you're lookin' fer who killed Ben Whittington . . ."

". . . when maybe you should be lookin' fer who killed Dan Carter."

He stared at the two brothers, saw the gleam of intelligence in their eyes. They were far from dumb shit-kickers, but they apparently never let on to the rest of the town.

He wondered if Ben Whittington knew how smart these guys were. Or if he considered them his dumb shit-kicker friends.

"Okay," Clint said, "so you're telling me you know who killed Dan Carter?"

"Nope," Clem said, "we ain't sayin' that at all."

"We're just sayin' Carter weren't liked by everybody in town."

"You got any idea who disliked him enough to kill him?"

"Have you talked to the folks who run things?" Clem asked.

"You mean like the town council?"

"Sure," Delbert said, "and maybe the mayor."

"Dan Carter owned a business in town," Clem said, "and he wanted to be a—whatayacallit?—town father."

"Look around town," Delbert said.

"That's all we're sayin'."

Clint studied the two brothers. Suddenly, there was a distance in their eyes, as if they were able to turn their intelligence on and off.

"Okay," Clint said, "thanks for the drink."

He stood up, then swayed a minute before catching himself on the table.

"Mash is kinda strong," Clem said.

"Gotta be careful," Delbert said.

"Yeah," Clint said, "I see what you mean. Thank you, boys."

"Good luck, Mr. Gunsmith," Clem said.

"Let us know if you find out who killed them two ol' boys," Delbert said.

"Yeah," Clint said. "I'll do that."

THIRTY

It was getting dark when Clint got back to Griggsville. He put Eclipse up at the livery and walked to the saloon. He entered and approached the bar. The place was about half full, but two men entered right behind him, so it was continuing to fill.

"Beer, Eddie," he said.

"Comin' up, Mr. Adams."

Hearing his name, two men standing at the bar moved farther away. Eddie came and set down his beer.

"Eddie, what can you tell me about Dan Carter?" Clint asked.

"Dan was an okay guy," Eddie said. "He ran his shop, came in here at night and drank."

"What about him and Adele Whittington getting married?" Clint asked. "Was he happy about that?"

"Why are you askin' me that?" Eddie asked.

"You're the bartender," Clint said. "You know everything."

Eddie looked pleased.

"Well, I don't know everythin'," Eddie said, "but I know Dan didn't wanna to get married."

"Then why was he?"

"He didn't know how to tell Ben Whittington no."

"Was he afraid of Whittington?"

"That's hard to say," Eddie said. "I don't know if it was fear, but somethin' was makin' him marry Adele."

"Until he disappeared the day of the wedding."

"Right."

"And then Whittington stormed off, and later they're both found hanging from a tree."

"If you're gonna ask me if I know who killed 'em," Eddie said, "the answer is no."

Clint sipped his beer and looked around.

"Any friends of Carter's in here now?" he asked.

"You know," Eddie said, "he drank in here, but he didn't really talk to anybody but me."

"And Whittington?"

"When he came to town, he had a drink," Eddie said, "but the only people I ever saw him talkin' to was those crazy Dagen brothers."

"Are they crazy?"

"Oh, yeah. You ever met them?"

"Yes," Clint said, "I've talked to them."

"They know who killed Whittington?"

"No."

"Well," Eddie said, "you really can't believe anythin' they say. And another thing . . ."

"What?"

"Don't drink their mash. It'll make you go blind."

"Thanks for the warning."

Clint left the saloon after one beer and started back to his hotel, but halfway there he decided to go somewhere else and changed direction.

He walked to Dan Carter's hardware store and tried the front door. It was locked. The sheriff must have seen to it that it was locked.

He remembered that someone had said that Carter lived above the store. He decided to walk around the building to find a way in. Maybe something in Carter's home would help him figure out what happened.

He walked around to the back and found a flimsy back door. He pressed his shoulder to it, shoved, and the door gave way. Inside he let his eyes adjust to the dark, then saw that he was in the storage room. If Carter lived upstairs, there had to be a stairway somewhere.

He found it in the shadows, and slowly made his way up. It was darker still up there, but eventually he was able to make out shapes. He groped, found a lamp on a table, and decided to light it. If the sheriff spotted the light on his rounds and showed up, he'd just explain.

He lit a match, got the lamp going, and the room was bathed in yellow light. He was in a room with an old sofa and table, and against a wall was an old stove. There was a doorway that led to a second room, where he found an unmade bed. Only two rooms, but there was everything a man could need there.

He went through both rooms, looking for anything

helpful. However, Dan Carter didn't seem to keep anything where he lived. There were no papers, no files. He must have had a desk or office downstairs for business. Clint had not done a thorough search of the hardware store his first time there, so he decided to go back down and take the lamp with him to light the way.

He went down the steps, and halfway down there was a shot. The bullet slammed into the wall as he dropped to the floor. Somebody ran out the back door, but he had dropped the lamp and a small fire had started. He had two choices. Chase the shooter and let the building burn down, or put out the fire.

He looked around for something to beat the flames with.

THIRTY-ONE

The fire might have gotten out of hand, but somebody had seen the flame and several more men showed up to help Clint put out the fire.

They had the flames out by the time the sheriff arrived.

"What the hell happened?" Bricker asked.

"It was my fault," Clint said. "I was having a look around. Somebody took a shot at me and I dropped a lamp."

"Who was the shooter?" Bricker asked.

"I don't know," Clint said. "Maybe the same shooter from this morning, but I didn't get a look at him either time."

"He must have been usin' a handgun this time," Bricker said.

"He was."

"Well then, he ain't been a very good shot with either one, has he. Short or long gun?"

"You're right, he hasn't," Clint said.

"Seems to me," Bricker said, "somebody just ain't tryin' that hard to actually hit you."

"Maybe," Clint said, "somebody's just trying to keep me interested."

"You mean they just don't want you to leave town?"

"Maybe. Look, can you get me in to see the mayor tomorrow?"

"The mayor?"

"Yeah, and the other members of the town council," Clint added. "I'd like to talk to all of them."

"About what?"

"About the killings."

The sheriff frowned.

"What do you think they'll know about the killings?" he asked.

"I won't know that until I ask them," Clint said, "will I?"

"I guess not." Bricker looked around. "Let's get out of here."

"I could use a beer," Clint said.

"Yeah, me, too," the lawman said. "Okay, everybody out!" he yelled.

The other men turned and looked at Clint and Bricker.

"And thank you," Clint added, "to all of you. Come on, the beer's on me."

THIRTY-TWO

Clint and Bricker took the other three men into the saloon and Clint bought them all a beer.

"What the hell went on?" Eddie asked. "You all look like crap and smell like soot."

"That's because we were fightin' a fire," one of them said.

"Where?"

"The hardware store," another said.

"Dan Carter's store?" Eddie asked. "Who started a fire there?"

"It was an accident," the sheriff said. "But it's out now, with no great damage. Drink up!"

Clint appreciated the fact that the sheriff fielded the question and skirted it.

The three men who helped put out the fire finished their beers and left to return home. Clint bought the sheriff a second one.

"Are you thinking that someone on the town council killed Ben Whittington?" Bricker asked.

"I'm wondering who killed Dan Carter. He was a businessman in town, so he had some contact with the mayor and the council, right?"

"That's right."

"So it makes sense for me to talk to them," Clint said. "First thing in the morning okay with you?"

"Fine with me," Bricker said. "I guess we'll find out how it sits with our town fathers."

They each finished their second beer and then left the saloon. They split up, Bricker heading for his office and Clint going to his hotel. It was fairly early, but he didn't feel like any more beer, and there was nothing else to do in the saloon. He might as well get a good night's rest.

He was trying to read but with little success. He'd been shot at twice that day, and he didn't know if it was by the same person. Maybe one was a warning, and one was trying to kill him.

He walked to the window and looked down at the darkened street.

If it was the same person who shot at him both times, that meant they were keeping an eye on him, or following him. The shooter knew he was at the hanging tree, and knew he was in the hardware store. What bothered him was that somebody was following him without him knowing it.

He dimmed the light in the room and continued to

stare at the street. As his eyes adjusted, he couldn't see anyone standing down there.

If somebody wanted to kill him, why not come at him when he was in his room?

He left the light out, went back to the bed, and sat on it. He took his gun from his holster and sat with it in his lap.

Waiting . . .

Two hours later he heard someone walking down the hall. He was tired, but he had not nodded off even once, remaining alert. He gripped his gun and waited.

The footsteps continued, then stopped. Apparently, they were in front of his door. He pointed his gun at the door, waiting for it to slam open from a kick. Instead, someone tried the doorknob, attempting gently to turn it, but he had made sure the door was locked.

And then someone knocked.

Would they knock, and then fire at him through the door? Or wait until it was opened.

He got off the bed and flattened himself against the wall next to the door.

"Who is it?"

"Clint?" a woman's voice called. "It's Debra."

"Are you alone?"

"Yes, if course I'm alone."

If he opened the door, would she shoot him? He reached for the doorknob, unlocked the door, then turned the knob and let the door fall ajar. He peered out, saw only Debra, but there could have been someone else off to the side.

"Come on in."

"Clint?" she said, pushing the door open.

When she stepped inside, he quickly stuck his head out in the hall. Seeing there was no one there, he withdrew and shut the door, then turned up the lamp on the wall. She turned and stared at him.

"What's wrong?" she asked. "Did you think I was going to shoot you?"

"I didn't know who it was," he said. "Somebody took a shot at me again tonight."

"Where?"

"At the hardware store."

"Why were you there?"

"I was just looking for something—anything—that might help."

He walked to the bedpost and holstered his gun, then turned to face her. He was still dressed, except for his boots.

"Why are you here?"

"Well . . . I thought you'd know."

"Debra, where's Adele?"

"She's home, asleep."

"Are you sure?"

"Yes," she said. "She's sound asleep, and she will be 'til morning."

"Debra," he said, "this is not a good idea."

"You don't want me?" She was wearing a shawl, and lowered it now so he could see she was wearing a dress that showed her shoulders, and some cleavage.

"Of course I do," he said, "but someone might try to kill me tonight."

"Here? In your room?"

"Yes," he said, "thinking I'm asleep."

"So . . . you're waiting for them?"

"Let's just say I'm ready," he said. "So you have to go home."

"I could stay," she said. "I could help."

"No," he said, "if you stay, you could get hurt, or die." He walked to her and took her by the shoulders. Her bare skin burned his hands. "You have to leave."

He pulled her to him and kissed her soundly. She slid her hand down the front of his pants and grabbed him. He reacted immediately and began to swell.

"This is not the way to persuade me to go," she said, pressing her face to his shoulder. His nose was in her hair, and he inhaled.

"Believe me," he said, "it's not easy for me either."

He pushed her away.

"Okay," she said, "I'll go, but first . . ."

She grabbed for his belt.

"Debra—"

"I just need something, Clint," she said. She reached in and brought out his cock, all swollen and red. "So do you, I see."

"Debra—shit!" He dropped his pants to the ground and his erection sprang out at her.

She got to her knees and took him in both hands. She rubbed the palm of her right had over the swollen head of his cock. She wet it with her tongue, then took it in her mouth and began to suck it—just the head.

"Jesus . . ." he breathed.

"Mmm," she said, using her left hand to fondle his heavy balls. She began to suck him more fully, but instead of opening her mouth and taking him in, she pressed the head of his cock against her lips, then pushed past them into her mouth. Each time she did that, it was like an extra sensation.

She began to suck him more quickly, moaning and making wet noises. He wanted it to go on forever, yet he wanted it to end quickly so he could get her out of there. Finally, he exploded into her mouth, spurting almost painfully . . .

"All right," she said moments later, "but the next time I come to your door, you better let me in and be prepared for a long night."

"Oh, I'll let you in," he promised.

She walked to the door and put her hand on the doorknob.

"Wait," he said.

He grabbed his gun, went to the door, and opened it. He peered out again, saw that it was empty, and said, "All right. You can go."

"Remember," she said, "when this is over . . ."

"Don't worry," he promised, "I'll remember."

She went out into the hall, and he closed the door and locked it.

THIRTY-THREE

Clint sat in the dark the remainder of the night with his gun in his lap. When first light filtered through the window, he allowed himself to nod off, but only briefly. When he awoke, he stripped down, washed himself, then dressed again and left the room.

He went out onto the street and walked up one side of the town and down the other. He was sure he wasn't being followed, but this was such a small town somebody could have been watching him all the way.

He crossed the street and went to the church. Finding it empty, he walked to the door of Father Joe's office and knocked.

"Come!" his friend's voice called.

Clint opened the door and entered. Father Joe stood up from behind his desk and came around.

"Breakfast?" Clint asked.

"Why not? Mrs. Colton's?"

"Why not?" Clint repeated.

They left the church and started for Mrs. Colton's house.

"I heard you had some excitement last night."

"The shooting or the fire?" Clint asked.

"Both."

"The fire was my fault, I shouldn't have dropped that lamp."

"You were probably scampering for your life at the time."

"I was, but that's still no excuse. I almost burned the building down."

"Did you manage to find anything while you were in there?"

"No," Clint said.

"Mrs. Colton's is this way," Father Joe reminded him.

"I know, but I'm supposed to meet with the sheriff this morning. Let's see if he wants to have breakfast with us."

They headed for the sheriff's office.

"What are you doing with the sheriff today?" Father Joe asked.

"He's going to take me to meet the mayor, and the other members of the town council."

"What do you want with them?" Father Joe asked.

"It's been pointed out to me that maybe I'm looking into the wrong killing," Clint said.

"Dan Carter? I assumed he was killed because he got in the way."

"In whose way?"

"Whoever killed Whittington."

"What if it was the other way around?"

"Why would anyone want to kill Carter? He ran the hardware store."

"So what did Whittington do that was so different? What makes him more important?"

"He owns property," Father Joe said. "You know as well as I do that a lot of men have been killed over property."

"It's not much of a farm to be killed over," Clint pointed out.

They stepped up onto the boardwalk in front of the sheriff's office, and Clint opened the door.

"I wondered what happened to you," Bricker said from behind his desk.

"How about some breakfast before we get started?" Clint asked.

"On you?" Bricker asked.

"Of course."

The lawman reached for his hat and said, "Lead the way."

As always, Mrs. Colton was very welcoming, while the rest of the people in the place cast sideways glances at them.

"Am I wrong or are people lookin' at me funny?" Bricker asked.

"It's not you," Clint said. "It's me."

"Or me," Father Joe said.

"I don't care which one of you it is as long as it ain't me."

They all ordered steak and eggs from Mrs. Colton, who left them with a pot of coffee and three mugs.

"You hear about the fire?" Bricker asked Father Joe.

"I heard," Father Joe said. "And the shooting."

"I wonder if it's the same shooter, or if Clint here has two people after him. Of course, it could just be somebody's after your rep."

"I thought of that," Clint said, "but that's too much coincidence for my liking."

"So you feel sure it has somethin' to do with these other killin's?"

"Yes, I do."

"Well then," Bricker said, "I guess after breakfast we'll walk over and see the mayor."

"Suits me," Clint said.

"You fellas mind if I come along?" Father Joe asked.

"I don't mind," Clint said.

"Whatever you want, Father," Bricker said. "You're the vicar, and I'm only the sheriff."

THIRTY-FOUR

Mayor Howard Tilton watched the three men file into his office. He sat back in his chair, a well-dressed man in his late fifties.

"Sheriff," he said, "Vicar . . . and this must be Clint Adams, who I've been hearing so much about."

"Yeah, this is Clint Adams, Mayor," Bricker said. "Clint, this is Mayor Howard Tilton. Mr. Mayor, Clint had been helping me try to find out who killed Ben Whittington and Dan Carter and hung them from a tree outside of town. And he has some questions for you."

"Well, anything I can do to help find out who killed two of our citizens, I'll be happy to do. What's on your mind, Mr. Adams?"

"It's Dan Carter, Mayor," Clint said. "As a businessman in town, was he ever a member of the town council?"

"Never."

"Did he want to be?"

"He and I had discussed it, yes. But the other members

of the council did not see him being fit," Tilton said. "Not yet anyway."

"What kept him from being fit?"

"Well, for one thing, he wasn't married."

"And are all the members of the council married?" Clint asked.

"They are," the mayor said, "and they are God-fearing, churchgoing men, as the vicar can attest to."

Clint looked at Father Joe, who shrugged and nodded.

"Dan Carter just didn't fit in," the mayor said.

"Could that be why he was getting married?" Clint asked.

"Could be," the mayor said.

"He didn't discuss with you if getting married would get him on the council?"

"As I said, we talked about it, but there was no guarantee."

"And what about Ben Whittington?"

"Whittington lived outside of town," the Mayor said. "There was never any question of him being on the town council."

"So maybe he just wanted to have a son-in-law on the council, then."

"Maybe," the mayor agreed.

"So killing both of them kept that from happening."

"I don't know of anyone," the mayor said, "who would kill just to keep Carter off the council. This is a small town, Mr. Adams. It's just not that important."

In Clint's experience, the size of the town didn't matter when it came to politics. Everything was a stepping-stone.

"Mayor, you don't have a problem with me talking to the other council members, do you?"

"I can't see any reason why I would," the mayor said. "The sheriff can take you to see each of them. But I can't believe that one of them may have killed these two men."

"In my experience, Mayor," Clint said, "anybody is capable of murder."

"I believe that," Tilton said, "but there still has to be a reason, and I just can't see one here. But I do have one thing to tell you, sir.

"What's that?" Clint asked.

"I appreciate the fact that you're staying in town to help the sheriff with this investigation."

"I happened to be here when the murders took place, Mayor," Clint said, "and I found the bodies. I feel I should see it through."

"Well, I hope you'll both solve this thing soon," the mayor said. "People in town just don't feel safe."

As they left, the mayor said good-bye, then actually came out from behind his desk to shake hands with Father Joe.

"Good to see you, Father."

"I expect to see you in church, Mayor."

"Definitely, Father. My wife and I will be there."

Father Joe followed Clint and the sheriff out.

"You want to come with us to see the others, Father Joe?" Clint asked.

"No," Father Joe said. "I have some of my own duties to perform. But I wish you luck, and hope you find out something that will help."

"So do I," Clint assured him.

Clint and Bricker watched Father Joe walk away, and then Clint said. "Looks like the mayor has a lot of respect for Father Joe."

"His wife likes the vicar," Bricker said. "In fact, most of the women in town do. They approve of the changes he's made. I'm sure you've heard that."

"Yeah, but I also see how much the people fear him," Clint said.

"Well," Bricker said, "you know his background."

"I wasn't aware the people in town did."

"Everybody knows he used to be a gunfighter named Joe Holloway," the sheriff said. "Everybody knows he can probably still use a gun. In fact, he probably still has his."

He did, Clint knew, because he had seen it, but he didn't say anything.

"It's not like he's been seen wearing it," Clint said.

"Not that I know of," the sheriff said, "but I wouldn't want to be the reason he put it back on. Come on, let's start seeing the council. Adam Weaving will be first."

"Where is he?"

"He owns the saloon."

"I thought Eddie owned the saloon."

"No, Eddie's just the bartender."

They started walking.

"Tell me something?"

"Sure," Clint said, "what?"

"Father Joe," Bricker said, "how good was he with a gun?"

"Damned good," Clint said. "One of the fastest I've ever seen."

"Really? That good? One of the best?"

"I didn't say one of the best," Clint told him. "I said one of the fastest."

THIRTY-FIVE

Weaving had an office in the back of the saloon.

"Is he in?" the sheriff asked Eddie.

"Yeah, he's there."

"Why have I never seen this man?" Clint asked.

"He never comes out while the saloon is open," Eddie said.

"Why not?"

Eddie shrugged.

"He's never told me," he said. "Maybe if you ask him, he'll tell you."

"Come on," Bricker said to Clint. "I'll introduce you."

They walked to the back of the empty saloon. They had to knock to be admitted by Eddie, who had offered them a beer.

"Too early," the sheriff said.

"Later," Clint said.

Bricker knocked on a door and opened it.

"Come in, Sheriff," Adam Weaving said. "I've been expecting you—the both of you."

"Did somebody tell you we were comin'?" Sheriff Bricker asked.

"No," Weaving said, "but I was expecting both of you anyway."

Clint entered behind Bricker and pulled the door closed. Weaving stood, but remained behind his desk. He was wearing a gambler's black suit and boiled white shirt, looked to be about forty.

"Clint Adams, the Gunsmith, I presume?"

"That's right."

Now he came out from behind his desk and extended his hand.

"Adam Weaving," he said, and they shook hands. "I was expecting that you would have some questions for me. Am I right?"

"You are."

"Then have a seat," Weaving said, "and ask away."

He walked back around behind his desk and sat down. Clint also sat, while the sheriff remained standing.

"You knew both Ben Whittington and Dan Carter," Clint started.

"Of course I did. Carter was a businessman in town, and Whittington came in here from time to time."

"How did you get along with Carter?"

"Fine, as far as I know."

"Did he hold it against you that you and the others kept him off the town council?"

"Oh, I suppose he was angry for a while," Weaving said, "but he knew what he had to do."

"Get married?"

"Well . . . that was one thing," Weaving said. "Certainly getting married would not have assured him of a place."

"But it would have helped."

"Yes."

"So he never made any threats against anyone you knew of?"

"No."

"And nobody on the council had any reason to want either man dead?"

"My God, no!" Weaving said. "Is that what you're doing now? Looking for a council member to pin these murders on?"

"We're not lookin' to pin these killin's on anybody, Mr. Weaving," Bricker said. "We're just tryin' to solve them."

"Well, I can tell you, you're looking in the wrong place now. Did you speak with the mayor?"

"We did," Clint said.

"And he sent you here?"

"No," Clint said, "I asked the sheriff to help me question the mayor, and the council. I still have to talk to the others."

"Well, I'm sure you'll hear the same thing from them that you're hearing from me," Weaving said.

"I have to talk to them anyway," Clint said, standing. "I appreciate your time."

"Of course," Weaving said, also standing. "Anything I can do."

He remained behind his desk while Clint and Bricker left the room.

They waved to Eddie the bartender on the way out, then stopped just outside the batwing doors.

"Where to now?" Clint asked.

"Three more," Bricker said. "Cecil Jones owns the hotel you're stayin' in. He's the closest one to here."

"Okay, then," Clint said. "Cecil Jones."

Bricker nodded. They stepped down into the street and headed for the hotel.

In his office Adam Weaving was sitting behind his desk, going over the exchange in his head. He wondered if it was time for the town council to meet again and discuss this new development.

THIRTY-SIX

In the hotel the desk clerk told them that Mr. Jones was on the top floor, supervising some work that was being done. Clint and Bricker thanked him and took the stairs to the third floor.

"There are no rooms for rent up here yet," Bricker said. "They're tryin' to get it ready to open."

"Why would they need another floor in a town this size?" Clint asked.

"I guess they're hopin' the town will grow some," the sheriff said.

At the end of the hall Clint saw a tall, gangly man with sandy hair, a hawk nose, and a bow tie. As they got closer, he saw that the man was in his forties. He was talking to another man, who was holding a hammer.

"Mr. Jones," the sheriff called.

The man looked, recognized Bricker, and said, "Oh, Sheriff. What can I do for you?"

"This is Clint Adams," Bricker said. "He's helping me

investigate the killin's of Bed Whittington and Dan Carter. He has some questions for you."

"For me? Why? I don't know anything about any killings," Jones said.

"I'm questioning everyone on the town council, Mr. Jones," Clint said. "There's no reason for you to take this personally."

Jones looked at the man with the hammer and said, "Give me a minute."

"Yeah, sure."

The man with the hammer went through the open door of a room and Jones turned to face Clint and Bricker.

"Go ahead," he said.

Clint asked pretty much the same questions he'd asked Weaving, and got the same answers. Jones didn't know any reason why anyone would want to kill either of the dead men.

"I didn't particularly care if Carter was put on the council or not," Jones said. "In fact, he could've replaced me, for all I care."

"Is that a fact?"

"I've got a hotel to run," Jones said. "I can't be running to meetings every time one of those bastards has a problem. And if you're talking to all of them, you can tell them I said so."

"Maybe I'll do that," Clint said.

"Fine. Can I get back to work now?"

"Sure," Clint said. "Thanks for your, uh, help."

"Whatever."

He went into the same room the man with the hammer

had gone into and they started talking again. Clint and Bricker went back down to the lobby.

"Funny," Clint said.

"What is?"

"Well, if they're working so hard to get that extra floor ready to be occupied," Clint said, "I sure haven't heard any hammering when I'm in my room."

"They probably ain't hammerin' at night."

"Probably not."

They went outside.

After Clint and Bricker left the hallway, Cecil Jones came back out and stared down the hall. Goddamn it, he thought, now he *was* going to have to meet with all those bastards again. God, but he hated town council meetings, especially since the mayor was always there.

"Mr. Jones?" the man with the hammer called. "What about this ceiling?"

"Just make sure it doesn't fall on anyone," Jones said. "I'll talk to you later."

THIRTY-SEVEN

Clint had basically the same conversation with the other two members of the council, Wade Philips, owner of the Feed & Grain, and Ted Swisher, owner of the livery stable. Neither of them was as well spoken or seemed as educated as Weaving and Jones.

"So, now what?" Bricker asked. "You talked to the mayor and all four members of the council. What did that tell you?"

"I get the feeling these last two just follow the votes of the first two."

"I think you're right," Clint said. "The mayor, Weaving, and Cecil Jones pretty much run the town."

"So if the deaths of those two men somehow benefited the town, we'd have to suspect one, two, or all three of them."

"I guess that's right."

They started walking back toward Sheriff Bricker's office.

"What about that idea of yours about federal help?" Bricker asked.

"What bothers me is that someone tailed me when I left town and I never saw them," Clint said.

"Well, this time you could be watchin' for them."

"I don't know," Clint said. "I think I'm close to something."

"You think you can solve this without any help?" Bricker asked.

"I think so," Clint said.

"I just hope there's no more killin's," the lawman said.

"So far the only other person who's been shot at is me," Clint pointed out. "It doesn't seem that anyone else in town is in danger."

"I hope you're right."

They reached the office and stopped in front.

"Coffee?" Bricker asked.

"I don't think so," Clint said. "I've got to go and do some thinking."

"Well," Bricker said, "I'll be here. Somethin' occurs to you, let me know."

"Same goes for you, Sheriff," Clint said.

"I don't think anythin's gonna occur to me," the sheriff admitted. "I'm just a sheriff, not a detective. I'm countin' on you, and so's the rest of the town."

Well, Clint thought, as long as there's no pressure.

Instead of going back to his hotel, or to the saloon, Clint decided to once again stop at St. James Church. If it wasn't for Father Joe, he wouldn't be in this predicament, with everyone counting on him to solve two murders.

When he walked into the church, he saw Father Joe sitting in one of the pews, talking to a man. As he got closer, he realized the man was Adam Weaving, the owner of the saloon.

"Am I interrupting anything?" he asked.

Both men looked up at him. Father Joe was calm, but Weaving looked surprised. He also looked like a man who had been caught with his hand in the till.

"No, no interruption," Father Joe said. "Mr. Weaving and I were just discussing future plans for the church. Have the two of you met?"

"We have," Clint said.

"Yes," Weaving said, standing up, "Mr. Adams came to my office and questioned me about the two murders."

"Ah, that's right," Father Joe said to Clint. "You told me you were going to question the members of the council."

"And I did."

"Did you get anything more out of the rest of them than you did from me?" Weaving asked.

"No, as a matter of fact," Clint said. "I got the same answers."

"That's what I thought," the saloon owner said.

"Thank you for your time, Mr. Weaving," Father Joe said.

"My pleasure, Father," Weaving said. "We'll talk further about the things you, uh, need."

Weaving nodded to Clint, and left.

"The things you need?" Clint asked.

"Money," Father Joe said, running his thumb together with his index and middle fingers.

"It's always about money, isn't it?"

"It is for this church," Father Joe said. "Was that true?"

"Was what true?"

"You got all the same answers from the members of the council?"

"And the mayor," Clint said, "yes."

"Like they planned it?"

"Like somebody planned it," Clint said. "Apparently, the town is run by the mayor with two of the council members, Weaving and Jones."

"True," Father Joe, "if you need to get anything done in this town, you have to see them."

"You've got to help me, Joe."

"What can I do?"

"The wedding," Clint said. "You were involved with the arrangements. Whose idea was the wedding, Whitington's or Carter's?"

"Well," Father Joe said, "that was an odd one. Usually, a wedding is arrangement by the mother and the bride."

"Not this one?"

"No," Father Joe said, shaking his head. "It was Whitington himself who came in, and a couple of times Carter came in with him to make the plans."

"Did they seem to get along?"

"It seemed to me they were like-minded in this," Father Joe said.

"So then why did the groom come to see you the day

before, all upset, and why did he disappear the day of the wedding?"

"Damned if I know, Clint," Father Joe said, "and I've been wondering about it since it happened."

"Have you talked to the two ladies about it?" Clint asked.

"No, I haven't," Father Joe said, "and I should go out there and check on them. Those poor women . . ."

Clint decided not to let Father Joe know that the ladies in question weren't really all that upset by the incidents of the past few days.

"Yup," he said, "poor women."

THIRTY-EIGHT

Clint realized he'd made a mistake. When stopping to talk to all the members of the town council, he had neglected to ask if he could examine their rifles. Still, he doubted any of those businessmen could have followed him without being seen, and taken that shot at him by the hanging tree, even though the shot missed. No, they would have had to hire that done.

Clint went to the saloon, ordered a beer from Eddie.

"I've got a question for you," he said when Eddie came with the beer.

"What's on your mind?"

"You know anybody in town who's a good shot with a rifle?"

Eddie stroked the bristle on his jaw.

"You don't fool me none," he said.

"I don't."

"No. You wanna know if there's anybody in town

who's a good shot with a rifle, who would hire himself out? Am I right?"

"You're right," Clint said. "And in addition to that, would he agree to bushwhack a man for money."

"This ain't Dodge City, Mr. Adams," Eddie said. "You ain't gonna find that kind of man here. Anybody in this town wants a killer, they gonna have to import him from out of town."

"Who in town has got the money to do that?"

Eddie shrugged, said, "Pretty much anybody on the town council. Maybe the mayor. They got money."

"Hmmm."

"Of course," Eddie went on, "there is a gunman who lives in town."

Clint studied the man, then said, "You mean an ex-gunman, right?"

Eddie shrugged again.

"You know better than me if a man can put down his gun for good," Eddie said.

"We're talking about Father Joe, right?" Clint asked.

"He's the only ex-gunman I know of in town," Eddie said.

Clint studied on the suggestion over his beer. Father Joe had invited him to town to see him in his new life. Knowing Clint was coming, why would he decide to kill two men? It didn't make sense.

But then none of this made sense. A would-be groom and would-be father-in-law were killed and hung from a tree. And nobody wanted them dead.

Clint remembered that somebody—Eddie?—had told

him about two gamblers who might have wanted to kill Ben Whittington after they accused him of cheating at cards. He had not followed up on those two names.

He waved Eddie over . . .

Eddie told Clint the two men who had accused Whittington of cheating were ranch hands, working on different ranches in the area.

Clint left the saloon and went back to the sheriff's office.

"So soon?" Bricker said as he entered. "What did you find out?"

"I've got two names, men who played poker with Ben Whittington and accused him of cheating. You know anything about that?"

"Doesn't ring a bell," the lawman said. "When did this happen?"

"About six months ago."

"Whew," Bricker said, "that's even before Father Joe came here."

"So there was poker going on then."

"Yeah."

"When did it stop?"

"About . . . four months ago."

"Why would one or two guys hold a grudge for six months and then act on it?"

"I don't know," Bricker said. "Would they?"

"I need to ask them. Do you know Tommy Reasoner or Frank Washburn?"

"The names aren't familiar."

"Well, they work—or worked—at the Bar Double-K and the 3W's ranches."

"Well," Bricker said, "I know where those are. Want me to—"

"Yeah," Clint said, "I do."

They left and walked to the livery to saddle their horses.

As they rode out of town, Clint said, "Eddie says he hasn't seen either man in town for a while."

"So we may be ridin' out to see two men who ain't even there anymore?"

"Maybe."

"Great."

THIRTY-NINE

Tommy Reasoner worked at the Bar Double-K, and he was still there.

"Yeah," he said, "I did want to kill Whittington—that night. He was cheatin'. Me and Frank both knew it."

"So why didn't you kill him that night?" Clint asked.

Reasoner stared at him. He was in his thirties, wasn't wearing a gun, but was wearing gloves because they had found him working fences.

"Because I ain't a killer," Tommy said. "Neither was Frank."

"So you just swallowed your anger and forgot about it?"

"We didn't exactly forget about it, but we both went back to work, didn't get back to Griggsville, never ran into Whittington again."

"Did you know him before that night?"

"No."

"And you never saw him again?"

"No."

"Why haven't you been back to Griggsville?"

"I heard they don't have girls or cards in the saloon anymore, thanks to some priest or somebody," Reasoner said.

"So where do you go to drink and play cards?" Clint asked.

"Clarksville, mostly. Sometimes Shipley, which is a little further away."

"When was the last time you were in Griggsville?" Bricker asked.

Reasoner thought about it for a moment, then said, "Geez, probably that night. Yeah, I ain't been back since then."

"What about your buddy?" Clint asked.

"Who?"

"Frank Washburn?"

"Frank's dead."

"What?"

"Yeah," Reasoner said, "four months ago."

"How?" Bricker aside. "Was he shot?"

"Naw," Reasoner said, "his horse fell on him, busted him up inside. Lasted a couple of days, but he finally died."

Clint looked at Bricker, who shrugged.

"I never heard anythin' about it," he said.

"Did he have a doctor?" Clint asked.

"There wasn't no doctor in Griggsville, which is the closest town," Reasoner said. "His boss sent somebody for the doctor in Clarksville, but he was out somewhere deliverin' a baby. By the time he got to Frank, it was too late."

"We have a doctor now," Bricker said lamely.

"Have you got a rifle?" Clint asked.

"Of course I do."

"Been fired recently?"

"Yeah," Reasoner said. "Me and a buddy shot some deer a week ago."

There was no point in checking the rifle, then.

"Say, what's this about?" Reasoner asked.

"You ain't heard?" Bricker said. "Two men in Griggsville were killed. Whittington was one of them."

"Yer kiddin'," Reasoner said. "Are you tellin' me you think I killed a man six months after I caught him cheatin' at cards? That's crazy."

"Yeah, well," Clint said, "we're just trying to be thorough."

"Well, I didn't kill nobody."

Clint believed him.

FORTY

Clint and Sheriff Bricker rode back to town, no wiser than when they'd left. They left their horses in the livery and walked to the church. They found Father Joe doing something at the altar. He turned as they entered.

"Find out anything?" he asked.

"One of the men we went to see died four months ago," Clint said. "The other one didn't do it."

"You're sure?"

"Positive."

"Then you're back where you started."

"Except that I need a beer, and so does the sheriff," Clint said. "Join us?"

"Sure," Father Joe said. "I can finish cleaning this later."

They left the church and headed for the saloon.

It was late afternoon now, but the saloon only had about half a dozen customers in it. They turned and looked as the three men entered the place. The two men standing at the bar moved to a far end.

"Don't worry," Clint said, slapping the lawman on the back, "it's still me."

"Or me," Father Joe said.

"Three beers, Eddie," the sheriff said.

"Comin' up."

Eddie lined three beer mugs up in front of them.

"Find them boys you was lookin' for?" he asked.

"One of them," Clint said. "The other one died four months ago."

"That's too bad."

"The one we found didn't do it," Sheriff Bricker said. "At least, that's what he said, and Mr. Adams here believed him."

"Didn't you?" Clint asked.

"Ah, yeah, I did."

"Back where you started, huh?"

"That's what I said," Father Joe replied.

"Well, my boss wanted to know when you fellas came in again," Eddie said. "Okay if I go tell 'im?"

"Sure," Clint said. "Tell 'im."

Eddie went back to his boss's office to give him the word while the three men stood and drank their beers. Maybe Adam Weaving had thought of something useful.

Eddie came out moments later, followed by Weaving.

"Well, gents, welcome," he said. "Eddie, I'll have what they're having."

"Yes, sir."

"How is your investigation going?" Weaving asked.

"Not well," Clint said.

"I'm sorry," Weaving said, accepting a beer from Eddie. "I was hoping you'd make some progress."

"Well," Clint said, "we've determined that two men didn't do it. I guess that's some kind of progress."

Nobody commented.

"Isn't it?"

Still, nobody commented.

Then Father Joe said, "Yeah, sure it is."

"What about the members of the council?" Weaving asked. "Have you found any of them with a motive to kill Whittington and Carter?"

"No," Clint said. "I can't see that any of you had a motive."

"Okay, then," Weaving said, "at least that's progress."

"I guess so," Clint said.

The sheriff looked around the saloon, then back at his comrades.

"The killer could be in here," he said. "He could be anywhere in town."

"At least it's a small town," Clint said.

"Small consolation, I say," Father Joe said.

Weaving looked around while they were finishing their beers.

"Sorry we're killing your business," Clint said.

"Oh, you're not," Weaving said. "We haven't had much since Father Joe here changed everything."

"They'll come back," Father Joe said. "Once they realize they don't really need the women and the gambling."

"You really think men are going to admit that to themselves?" Weaving asked.

"Yes, I do."

Weaving put his beer down, one third of it still in the mug.

"You fellas have another, on the house," he said. "I have to go back to work."

"I do, too," Bricker said as Weaving walked away, "but I'll have another."

Clint looked at Father Joe, who said, "Why not?"

FORTY-ONE

Outside the saloon they split up. Sheriff Bricker went back to his office, while Clint walked Father Joe back to St. James Church.

"You know what still bothers me?" Clint asked.

"What?"

"The fact that somebody followed me without my knowing it," he said.

"What's so unusual about that?"

"It's never happened before."

"Never?"

"Never," Clint said, "at least, not by somebody other than an Indian."

"You're saying it takes an Indian to track you?" Father Joe said.

"Track, follow . . . sneak up on."

He snapped his fingers and pointed at Father Joe.

"What?" the vicar asked.

"What do you know about the Dagen brothers?"

"I know that you said you talked to them and they didn't do it," Father Joe said.

"Yeah, but I just realized something."

"What?"

They stopped in front of the church.

"When I got there, Delbert—I think it was Delbert—came out of the house and pointed a gun at me."

"So?"

"So then Clem—at least, I think it was Clem—came up behind me—and I didn't hear him."

"So you're saying the Dagen brothers are part Indian?" Father Joe said.

"I'm saying they're light on their feet," Clint said. "Maybe too light."

"Did you check their guns?"

"Yeah, but maybe not all of their guns," Clint said. "I think I'm going to have to go out there and pay them another visit."

"You want some company?"

"Are you going to bring your Bible?"

"I am," Father Joe said. "Just let me go and get it, and then we can saddle our horses."

"Okay," Clint said. "Okay, maybe a Bible will come in handy. Who knows?"

They rode to within sight of the Dagen place and reined in.

"How do you want to play this?" Father Joe asked.

"Well, since I have a gun and you have a Bible, I thought I'd go first."

"And what do I do?"

"You make sure Clem doesn't sneak up on me again."

"I can do that."

They dismounted, and Clint handed Eclipse's reins to the vicar, then started toward the house.

While Father Joe kept a wary eye out for Clem, he opened his saddlebags, took out his rolled-up holster, unrolled it, and strapped it on.

"Welcome home," he said, adjusting the belt.

Clint got up to the house and moved alongside it. He peered in a window and saw that the house was empty. He walked to the front, opened the door, and stepped inside. Still empty. When he came out, Father Joe was approaching, leading their horses. Clint noticed the gun and holster on his hip.

"What's that all about, Father?" he asked.

"Better range than a Bible," Father Joe said. "I don't want someone shooting you while I'm throwing a Bible at them."

"I appreciate the thought."

"I checked the barn," Father Joe said. "Their horses are gone."

"I wonder where they went," Clint said.

"We could try tracking them," the vicar said. "There are a lot of tracks, but I'll bet you're still good enough to pick out the fresh ones."

"Suddenly," Clint said, "I've got an itch."

"Where?"

"Right in the middle of my back."

"You think they're out there right now, watching us?" Father Joe asked.

"Could be," Clint said. "If so, they're both damned good. Too good just to be a couple of dumb farmers. Although I don't think they're so dumb."

"So they act dumb to throw people off," Father Joe said. "And this place doesn't look like it makes any money, so how do they live?"

"Maybe," Clint said, "they put their special skills to use."

"Killing people?"

"Why not?"

"For money," Father Joe said.

"Otherwise, why would they feel the need to kill Whittington and Carter?" Clint asked.

"So somebody hired them."

"And we're back to trying to figure out who in town wanted those two men dead."

Suddenly, it got very quiet.

"I'm starting to feel that itch you were talking about," Father Joe said.

"I'll go left, you go right," Clint said. "And let the horses go."

"Okay."

"One . . . two . . ."

The first shot came before three.

FORTY-TWO

Father Joe let go of the horses, who moved away from the house. The animals had a great sense of self-preservation—especially Eclipse.

Clint dove right, and Father Joe dropped left. They both rolled and came up with their guns in their hands. To the vicar it felt like he'd never put the gun down.

"Where are they?" Clint asked.

"Can't see. They're a long way off."

"That shot came close," Clint said. "The horses were in the way."

"We can't give them a clean shot."

"No," Clint said, "but we've got to get closer. We can't do much damage from here."

"I can work my way around behind the barn," Father Joe said. "Maybe I can see something from there."

"I'll try for that stand of hackberry trees there," Clint said.

"Okay," Father Joe said. "On three?"

"Again?" Clint said. "Let's just . . . go!"

"I tolja we shoulda killed him when he came ta see us," Delbert said to Clem.

"Yeah, yeah. I tolja to aim a little to the left," Clem said.

"I ain't used ta missin'," Delbert said. "I don't even know why ya made me miss when he was at the tree."

"I thought killin' the Gunsmith would bring too much attention," Clem said. "How many time I gotta tell ya?"

"So now we gotta kill him and the vicar," Delbert said. "That ain't gonna bring too much attention to Griggsville, is it?"

"Time for us ta leave town anyway," Clem said, "get set up someplace else, start takin' jobs again."

"Killin' is all we're good at, Clem," Delbert said. "That and makin' mash." He licked his lips. "Sure wish I had me that jug now."

"We'll get the jug after we kill them," Clem said, "then we'll get outta town."

"Hey," Delbert said, "they're movin'."

"I'll take Adams," Clem said, "you take the priest."

"I gotta kill the priest?"

"Well, once of us gotta kill the priest."

"Why don't you do it?"

"You wanna take the Gunsmith?"

"Sure," Delbert said. "Why do you get to be the man who killed the Gunsmith?"

"You idiot, we ain't gonna tell anybody we killed him," Clem said. "And we ain't religious!"

"Yeah, well . . . I still don't wanna kill no priest."

"Fine," Clem said. "I'll take the priest, you take the Gunsmith."

"Okay."

"And you better not miss."

"I won't."

They split up.

Clint got to the stand of trees without drawing any fire. From the sound of it, Father Joe had also made it to the barn. If they each got close enough for their pistols to be effective, Clint felt they would have the upper hand. The Dagen brothers seemed to like to do their killing from a distance.

He remained in the trees, keeping silent and listening intently. Would the Dagens stay where they were, or try to move in?

He decided to wait and see . . .

Father Joe made it to the barn, moved around to the rear of it. From there he thought he could get an angle on the Dagens. He didn't know what he would do when he got within range. He hoped to be able to get the drop on at least one of them, and get him to drop his gun. If he had to use his gun for the first time in years, he didn't know if he'd be able to. And if he did, he didn't know how he would be able to justify it.

He peered around from behind the barn and saw that the Dagens had split up and were on the move. The justification would have to come later . . .

* * *

Clint was also wondering about Father Joe and whether or not he'd be able to use his gun. If not, then he was out here alone again two stone killers. But if Father Joe—the former gunfighter Joe Holloway—could not use a gun, why would he have offered to come and watch his back? He certainly knew that a Bible would not do the job.

Clint didn't hear anyone moving around, but the Dagens had already proven they could move without making a sound. He decided it was he who needed to move.

He turned, came out of the trees, and found himself facing Clem Dagen . . .

FORTY-THREE

Clem stopped short when he saw Clint come out of the trees. It was a shock because he thought he could get the drop on Clint.

He brought his rifle up . . .

Father Joe could tell what Delbert Dagen was aiming to do. He was going to come from the back of the barn, right where the vicar was. Father Joe backed away, ran to the other end, and ducked around the side just as Delbert made it to the back.

Father Joe flattened himself against the wall to wait, and did not draw his gun . . .

Clint saw Clem's rifle coming up, took the time to say, "Don't," but knew the man was committed. He had no choice but to draw and fire . . .

* * *

The sound of the shot did not surprise Father Joe. He was expecting shots. What surprised him was that there was only one.

He steadied himself, though, because he couldn't hear Delbert moving. The Dagens moved like Indians. But when the man appeared, Father Joe was ready . . .

Delbert heard the shot, but didn't react. He didn't like that the shot came from a pistol, but he had to concentrate on what he was doing. He hoped to come around the barn and be able to get the drop on the priest.

As he came around the barn, though, he saw the priest standing in front of him, his hand coming up. He brought the rifle up at the same time . . .

Clint's bullet hit Clem squarely in the chest. The man stepped back in surprise, looked down at the blood on his chest, then looked at Clint again. He opened his mouth to say something, but instead blood gushed from it, and he finally fell. Clint stepped to the body and kicked the fallen rifle away. Then he heard the shot.

From a rifle . . .

Father Joe brought the Bible up, realized that Delbert thought he had a gun. "Wait," he said, but Delbert triggered the rifle.

The bullet struck the Bible with a solid *thwack*, and went through it. The book was not thick enough to absorb the bullet, but it slowed it down. When it came out the other end, it struck Father Joe in the left arm, spinning him around and knocking him to the ground.

On his back the vicar of St. James watched as Delbert Dagen stepped forward and pointed the rifle down at him.

"I'm sorry, Father," the killer said.

"I forgive you," Father Joe said.

Delbert's finger was not on the trigger. In the split second it took him to put his finger on the trigger, Clint was there.

"Delbert!"

The killer looked up, saw Clint, and tried to lift the rifle and train it on him. Clint fired his second shot of the day and Delbert fell over backward, his rifle flying from his hand.

Clint moved quickly to kick the rifle away just in case, then bent over Father Joe.

"You all right?" he asked.

"I'm fine . . . just my arm . . ."

Clint pulled him to his feet, saw the Bible in his hand with the hole in it.

"Looks like you decided to go with the Bible after all."

"It saved my life," the vicar said. "Slowed the bullet down."

"Well, a bullet of your own would have saved your Bible."

"Maybe," Father Joe said, "but what would it have done to my soul?"

Clint shook his head and said, "Damn it, don't ask me questions I can't answer."

They heard a moan and looked down at Delbert.

"He's still alive," Father Joe said.

The vicar rushed to the fallen man's side and took his hand.

FORTY-FOUR

Clint and Sheriff Bricker entered the saloon and approached the bar. Once again men moved to be farther away from them.

"Hey, don't worry," the sheriff called out, "we got the men who tried to kill Adams."

That didn't seem to ease anybody's mind.

"Couple of beers, Eddie," the sheriff said.

"Comin' up," Eddie said.

He got the beers and set them on the bar.

"You got 'em?" Eddie asked.

"Clint and Father Joe did," Bricker said.

"The vicar?" Eddie asked.

"He didn't fire a shot," Clint said. "He did it with his Bible."

"So . . . they're in jail?" Eddie asked.

"Oh, no," Clint said, "they're dead. Father Joe used his Bible, and I used my gun."

"So why'd they do it?" Eddie asked.

"Do what?"

"Kill Whittington and Carter?"

"Oh, that was their business," Clint said. "Everybody thought they were a couple of dumb farmers, but they were actually hired killers."

"Those two?"

"Yup," Bricker said. "Turns out they were great shots with a rifle."

"Not much good close up, though," Clint added.

"Wow," Eddie said. "Too bad they're dead. It'd be nice to know who hired them."

"Oh, we know," Clint said, sipping his beer. "One of them lived just long enough to tell us. Seemed he thought it might ease his soul in the afterlife. At least, that's what Father Joe told him."

"So . . . he told you, huh?"

"Oh yeah, he did," Sheriff Bricker said, "and if you come out from under that bar with a shotgun, Eddie, I'll kill you."

Eddie looked at Clint.

"Oh, me, too," he said.

Eddie brought his hands out empty.

Clint turned to the few men who were in the saloon.

"Somebody better go and tell Weaving he needs a new bartender out here."

At the doctor's Clint found Father Joe with his arm in a sling, and bandaged.

"How's he doing, Doc?" Clint asked.

The physician, a young man who, oddly enough, had come to Griggsville to try and build a practice, said, "Oh, he'll be all right. The bullet missed the bone. That Bible really slowed it down."

"Can I take him out of here?"

"In a little while," the doc said. "I want him to rest some, and if I let him go, I know he won't."

He walked away and left them alone.

"Get him?" the vicar asked.

"Yeah, the sheriff's got him in his jail."

"Why'd he do it?"

"Well, seems the real owner of the saloon is Eddie," Clint said. "Weaving's just his front man. Eddie had some kind of land deal going with Whittington, which Carter found out about. He had Carter killed, but Whittington, drunk, stumbled into it and the Dagens killed him, too."

"Why'd they string them up like that?"

"Delbert said it was Clem's idea. 'It just come to him,' he said, and then he died."

"So it's all over."

"Yes."

"Somebody will have to tell those two poor women."

"Father Joe, those two women aren't so pathetic, believe me," Clint said.

"Are you gonna tell them?"

"No," Clint said, "I think that should come from you, Father." Clint didn't want to be around when the two women compared notes about him and realized he'd been with both of them.

"What are you gonna do?"

"Time for me to do what I started out to do," Clint said. "Leave."

Father Joe put out his right hand and they shook emphatically.

"Take it easy on your flock, Joe," he said. "They're afraid of you."

"I know," Father Joe said. "I'll ease their mind some. But do me a favor."

"What?"

"Skirt around that tree when you leave," Father Joe said, "just in case."

Clint grinned and said, "I'll do that."

Watch for

THE LAST BUFFALO HUNT

365th novel in the exciting GUNSMITH series
from Jove

Coming in May!